GW01465415

LONDON'S LEADING LADY

The Castleburys
Book 4

By Jennifer Seasons

DRAGONBLADE PUBLISHING, INC.

© Copyright 2024 by Jennifer Seasons
Text by Jennifer Seasons
Cover by Dar Albert

Dragonblade Publishing, Inc. is an imprint of Kathryn Le Veque Novels, Inc.
P.O. Box 23
Moreno Valley, CA 92556
ceo@dragonbladepublishing.com

Produced in the United States of America

First Edition July 2024
Trade Paperback Edition

Reproduction of any kind except where it pertains to short quotes in relation to advertising or promotion is strictly prohibited.

All Rights Reserved.

The characters and events portrayed in this book are fictitious. Any similarity to real persons, living or dead, is purely coincidental and not intended by the author.

ARE YOU SIGNED UP FOR DRAGONBLADE'S BLOG?

You'll get the latest news and information on exclusive giveaways, exclusive excerpts, coming releases, sales, free books, cover reveals and more.

Check out our complete list of authors, too!

No spam, no junk. That's a promise!

Sign Up Here

www.dragonbladepublishing.com

—⟫⟩⟨⟨—

Dearest Reader;

Thank you for your support of a small press. At Dragonblade Publishing, we strive to bring you the highest quality Historical Romance from some of the best authors in the business. Without your support, there is no 'us', so we sincerely hope you adore these stories and find some new favorite authors along the way.

Happy Reading!

CEO, Dragonblade Publishing

Additional Dragonblade books by Author Jennifer Seasons

The Castleburys Series
Mayfair Misfit (Book 1)
Duke Undone (Book 2)
Dockside Duchess (Book 3)
London's Leading Lady (Book 4)

CHAPTER ONE

October 1832
Tipton House
Mayfair, London

L OTTIE GLARED, BARELY restraining herself from lobbing the candleholder sitting next to her on the fireplace mantel toward the object of her fury. "Why must you continue to insist that this man is the best in the business?"

"Because he is."

"I can assure you that he is not." *She* was. That title decidedly belonged to her, even if none other than herself knew it.

Women cast no shadows in the theatre. Aside from those fortunate few blessed with a voice angelic enough to warrant a trip onto the stage at the Royal Opera House or Drury Lane. The rest of the female persuasion remained spectators, momentary travelers resting their laurels in cushioned velvet seats designed first and foremost for the privileged rich. The aristocracy. The *ton*. To which she, Lady Lottie, youngest daughter of the recently deceased seventh Earl of Castlebury, also belonged.

Now sister to the *eighth* Earl of Castlebury—the scoundrel currently vexing her greatly with his amused silence while the Duke of Somerton tried his blue-blooded best to drop her flat to the floor from a coronary fueled by internally combusted rage. Indeed, the very air in the drawing room of Tipton House suddenly felt quite stifling.

Lottie glared at her eldest brother, Crawford. "You're less than helpful, you know. Rather *unhelpful*, in truth."

"What am I to do when you and Rainville get bees in your bonnets about Thatcher Goodrich? Every blasted time that playwright's moniker is mentioned, you puff up like a peacock and begin squawking, providing Rainville the riotous entertainment he seeks."

Lottie lit up like a lightning storm at her sibling's words, offense and belittlement setting very ill upon her chest. Her head swiveled in a not dissimilar motion to an owl's, and her gaze stabbed her target with fierce, fiery daggers of indignation. "*Excuse me?*" she inquired.

"Mind your step, dear brother. This Castlebury has a tongue sharp as her sister's," Rainville advised with a tip of his regal chin toward Lottie, his honey-toned gaze sparking with humor. "Bleed you out if you don't keep a keen eye."

"And well I know it," Crawford muttered, raking a hand through his glossy auburn hair, disheveling it. "You married the nicest one," he groused, jutting his chin out stubbornly, no doubt preparing for Lottie's next verbal blow.

"*Nora* and *nice* are not words generally connected together within the same sentence." Rainville chuckled, his countenance alight with the love that he held for the middle Castlebury sister, now the Duchess of Somerton—and much adored by the wholly devoted and forever-smitten duke.

Lottie's gaze shifted between her brother and her brother-in-law, her frustration mingling with a sense of artistic injustice as she felt fuming and indignant. She was determined to prove herself in the world of theatre, even if it meant challenging the conventions of her time.

Thatcher Goodrich and his plays be damned.

"If women controlled the theatre industry, the quality of it would increase a thousand-fold, and the tales would be rather more sophisticated."

"Is that so?" Rainville smirked, always the smug duke.

"Yes, that's so." Oh, her spine veritably cramped from right-eous rigidity. "And you blooming well know it."

As the argument continued, Lottie's resolve only strength-ened. She would not be silenced or dismissed. Thatcher Goodrich might be the current darling of the theatre world, but Lady Lottie Castlebury was about to make her mark.

"Why, Rainville, must you always champion Goodrich?" Lottie questioned, her voice tinged with exasperation. "The man is no Shakespeare, and I shall not stand idly by while the world sings his praises as though he were. Not when I, a lowly female, find myriad shortcomings with the third acts of his plays—and can do exceedingly better at the task of creating them."

Rainville sighed dramatically, leaning against the mantelpiece. "Lottie, you've always been passionate about the theatre, and I admire your enthusiasm. But perhaps you're too quick to dismiss others' talents. Goodrich has a gift."

Lottie couldn't help but scoff. "A gift for mediocrity, perhaps. If the world wants to ignore the brilliant minds of women in the theatre, then so be it. But I refuse to let it pass unchallenged."

Crawford, ever the diplomat, attempted to interject. "Lottie, I understand your frustration. But sometimes, in order to change the world, one must first navigate it. You're a talented writer, but you need a platform, an opportunity. That's not easily afforded a woman today, more's the pity."

Lottie's gaze flicked between her brother and her brother-in-law. She knew they meant well, but their advice felt like chains, holding her back from her true potential. The world had always been a stage, and Lottie yearned to command it. Her jaw set with determination and her quiet blue eyes flashed. "Very well," she conceded, though her tone held a hint of defiance. "I shall seek my own opportunity, away from the confines of this stifling drawing room." With that, Lottie stormed through Tipton House, her violet skirts swirling in her wake, leaving Crawford and Rainville to exchange glances of concern.

She stomped out of Tipton House onto Grosvenor Square

with all the dramatic flair of a Shakespearean heroine betrayed, feeling rather satisfied with her theatrics. Her indignation was a tempest within her, churning with unyielding determination. The grandeur of the mansion's presence on the square dimmed in comparison to her fiery spirit.

The ornate ancestral portraits lining the walls of Tipton House had borne witness to generations of Castleburys who had adhered to the norms of aristocracy. But Lottie was different, an anomaly among her lineage—a woman fueled by dreams that transcended the limitations of her privileged existence. Well, perhaps not an *anomaly*, per se. Both her sisters fell far outside the realm of normal, expected behavior. Both defied conventions. So perhaps it was simply in their breeding as the daughters Castlebury.

The opulence of Grosvenor Square extended beyond the walls of Tipton House, but Lottie's thoughts were far from the splendor of the aristocratic neighborhood. Her heart raced with the turmoil of her emotions, and her determination was unwavering. She would not allow societal norms to stifle her artistic aspirations. Not when she knew beyond doubt that she was as good as any man.

As she stretched her legs in the cool London air, the city's bustling sounds greeted her. The cobbled streets of Mayfair stretched before her, winding their way through privilege and propriety. The weight of societal expectations pressed down on her shoulders, but she refused to bow to convention. With every stride, Lottie's thoughts swirled with plans and possibilities. She knew that she needed to seek her own opportunities, to carve out a path that would lead her to the stage she so dearly longed to command with her words. The theatre was her passion, her sanctuary, and she would let nothing stand in her way. But how to do it remained the looming question.

How?

Unbeknownst to Lottie, the old, frayed bag she currently clutched with frustrated fists against her side bore the brunt of her emotional turmoil. Its weathered seams finally surrendered to her twisting and rending, releasing her most treasured possession—her journal filled with the carefully crafted words of her plays. She unknowingly abandoned it somewhere amidst the delights of Grosvenor Square, losing it during her furious departure.

Lottie's inner fire burned brightly with each step, her heart a beacon of unwavering resolve. She had set her sights on a future where she would challenge conventions, shatter expectations, and prove that a woman's voice could command the spotlight. The stage awaited her, and she would claim it as her own, no matter the obstacles in her path. Rainville could take his fancy playwright and stuff a goose with him.

Her steps carried her further into Mayfair, where the city's elite mingled in grand ballrooms and exclusive clubs just beyond her view. Lottie marched along in her steady, capable way of moving. She would write her own destiny, just everyone wait and see.

"Goodrich could use some tutoring from the likes of me on how to create a moving and emotionally satisfying third act." Lottie scrunched her nose and glanced to the clouds, fluffy as sheep's wool as she grumbled, "But do I even get the chance? *Noooo*. What would a li'l miss like me know about script writing?"

As Lottie ventured farther from Tipton House, her footsteps echoed the rhythm of her racing heart. Crossing Park Street, she sighed as hard-packed road gave way to the inviting embrace of Hyde Park. The sprawling green expanse stretched before her, a sanctuary of nature in the heart of bustling London. A sense of serenity washed over Lottie as she entered the park, the weight of her recent confrontation gradually lifting as she meandered through the great park. The towering trees rustled their approval, their leaves whispering secrets that only she could understand. For Lottie, Hyde Park was more than just a place of leisure; it was her muse, her refuge.

She wandered along the winding paths, the vibrant colors of blooming flowers catching her eye. The air was crisp and invigorating, and the distant laughter of children playing added a touch of innocence to the surroundings. Lottie's mind, ever consumed by her passion for the theatre and written word, momentarily found solace in the simple beauty of the park.

Her old bag, a loyal companion on countless journeys, swung at her side as she strolled. She brushed her fingers against it briefly, knowing within were contents that held the hopes and dreams of a burgeoning playwright, the pages within her journal filled with her most cherished words. It had been her confidant, her creative partner in the creation of countless characters and stories.

As Lottie continued to meander through the park's winding trails, she became lost in her thoughts. Scenes from her latest play danced before her mind's eye, characters taking shape, their voices calling out to be heard. She was so engrossed in her creative reverie that she didn't notice the faint tearing of the frayed seams. It wasn't until she reached a secluded spot near a picturesque pond that she realized her journal was no longer in her possession.

"No!" she gasped. "No, oh please, no!" Panic seized her heart as she frantically patted her bag, searching for the familiar weight of her treasured notebook. But it was gone, lost somewhere amidst the serene beauty of Hyde Park. Or Park Street. Or Grosvenor Square.

Good God, it could be anywhere.

Her most private thoughts and feelings in play form.

Gone.

"Oh hellfire, what if someone finds it?" Lottie whispered, mortification heating her round cheeks. "What if they *read* it?"

Her hands trembled as she retraced her steps, scanning the path for any sign of her beloved journal. The park, once a source of solace, now felt like a treacherous labyrinth, hiding her most precious creation. Her breath quickened, and a sense of desperation washed over her. "Come on, come on," she urged quietly.

The world around her seemed to blur as she retraced her

path, searching for any trace of the lost journal. Every tree and every flower appeared to taunt her with its beauty, mocking her misfortune. She questioned the fates that had led her to this moment, one filled with frustration and heartache and preemptive humiliation. The things she had written in there! Oh, it was too much to bear.

A gentle breeze rustled, finally bringing Lottie back to the present, carrying with it the faint scent of ink and paper. She followed the breeze to the edge of the pond, where she spotted a few loose pages from her journal caught in the reeds. Her heart leaped with a mixture of relief and anguish as she gingerly retrieved the scattered remnants of her work. "There you are!" she squealed, snatching them up. "Well, there two of you are. But I'll take it."

The pages, though disheveled and damp from their encounter with the pond, still held her carefully penned words. How had they gotten there? Where in heaven's name were the rest? Lottie clutched them to her chest, a mix of gratitude and sorrow welling within her. While her journal was momentarily lost, she had salvaged a portion of her creativity, a glimmer of hope amidst the awful reality of her missing work.

As she sat by the pond, the setting sun casting a golden glow across the water, Lottie vowed to herself that this setback would not deter her. If she could not find her journal then she would re-create her lost work, breathing life back into her characters and stories. The theatre still beckoned, and she was determined to answer its call with renewed determination and unwavering passion.

Seated there, her skirts bunched around her, Lottie clutched the damp pages of her journal to her chest, her frustration and determination waging a silent battle within her. She stared out at the serene water, its surface rippling gently in the fading light of day. Birds chirped in the branches overhead. In this moment, she was alone and thankful for it. "I bet I left it in my bedchamber." Brightened by the idea, she stated it again. "That's it! You simply left it in your chamber. Why, it's not lost at all."

She almost believed herself.

In her welcome solitude, Lottie found herself muttering a conversation to an unlikely audience—a group of ducks that had gathered by the pond's edge. Her words spilled out, a mixture of exasperation and indignation. "Lousy, arrogant men, the lot of them," she grumbled. "Think they know everything, don't they? As if the world revolves around their opinions and accomplishments. As if they're the only ones who possess them."

The ducks, seemingly unfazed by her rant, continued to paddle lazily in the water, their quacks a gentle background chorus to her musings.

Lottie leaned closer to the pond, eyes narrowing as she continued her one-sided conversation. "They'll ignore your ideas, your dreams, or worse—claim them as their own. And what do we women get? Condescension and dismissal. A pat on the head. Told to look pretty, act affable but not too intelligent. Well, I won't stand for it any longer." She paused for a moment, her steely gaze fixed on the ducks, as if she were seeking their approval. "I'll show them. I'll prove that a woman's voice is just as powerful, just as deserving of recognition, as any man's. The theatre will be my stage, and I'll command it with my words. Thatcher Goodrich has rather the competitor in me, whether he yet knows it or not."

The ducks, indifferent to the weight of her declaration, paddled away in search of morsels beneath the water's surface. Lottie sighed, feeling a momentary connection with these feathered creatures, who seemed equally unimpressed by the world's injustices as they were to her fervent declarations. With renewed determination, she unfolded the salvaged pages of her journal and began to read her own words, her fingers tracing the ink-stained lines.

As the sun dipped below the horizon, casting the park in a soft, ethereal glow, Lottie whispered a promise to the fading light. "I'll write stories that will captivate hearts and minds, that will leave audiences breathless. And no man, no matter how lousy or arrogant, will stand in my way."

With her resolve strengthened, she gathered the scattered pages and carefully placed them back into her bag. Unbeknownst to Lottie, the tattered remnants of her journal were not as secure in her bag as she had hoped. As she carefully placed the ink-stained pages back into the weathered journal, she failed to notice the bag's pitiable condition. The bag, weakened by years of faithful service, had given way completely at the bottom, leaving a hole that gaped like a silent cry for help. Her pages passed swiftly and silently through.

Lottie hoisted her bag onto her shoulder, oblivious to the tragedy unfolding beneath her, the loose pages fluttering to the grass.

"I won't let anyone steal my voice, my stories," she declared with conviction, her words resounding through the park.

With a final quack of bemusement, the ducks retreated from the scene, leaving the scattered remnants of Lottie's dreams behind.

As she continued her journey through Hyde Park, the weight of her determination was palpable, and the loss of her journal remained a constant agitation, an anxiety. Her steps quickened, the need to find it safely within her chambers propelling her feet down the dirt path.

"Please let it be at home."

Otherwise, God help her.

CHAPTER TWO

T HATCHER GOODRICH STOOD amidst the sprawling expanse of
Hyde Park, his breath forming small clouds in the chilly
London air. His attire, a fashionable yet weathered ensemble,
hinted at a man who had seen his fair share of debauchery and
decadence in the city. A dark greatcoat, stylish but slightly frayed
at the edges, clung to his lean frame, while his black hair,
perpetually unruly, gave a stark contrast to the pale October sky.

The gloomy weather perfectly matched his moody disposition, and he grumbled to himself as he walked, a cloud of
discontent hovering over his thoughts. His cynical mind, ever
tainted by the theatre world's excesses, weighed him down like
an anchor in the murky sea of his writer's block.

His damned *writer's block*.

Blasted inconvenient, that.

People bustled around him, wrapped in their own worlds,
oblivious to his internal turmoil. Couples strolled hand in hand,
their laughter ringing in his ears, while children chased each other
through the park, their gleeful cries a stark contrast to his own
discontent. Thatcher found himself envying their carefree
innocence, a sentiment that only deepened his current frustration.

He trudged through the damp grass, the faint scent of earth
and the distant sound of a fountain serving as a reminder of the
natural world's resilience against the artifice of Society. It was a
stark contrast to the artificiality of the London theatres, where he

had spent most of his life. First as a young stagehand, and then later as an actor himself. Only after years of hard, grueling work had his talent with a pen paid off.

Now, he wrote. He created worlds with words. Emotions. *Lives.*

The pressure of it crushed meeker men.

With each step, his thoughts circled back to King William's recent request—a new play, a blank canvas he couldn't fill. The weight of expectation bore down on him, and he muttered to himself, his words a testament to his desperation. "I can't disappoint the king, not now." Not when he'd finally made something of himself—the lowly fifth son of a wastrel, an impoverished baron who'd chosen a quill for his weapon instead of the sword as his brothers had done. With four in line for the title before him, he'd fended much for himself. Learned to depend upon himself for survival. His words, his mind, had been his dagger.

Now it refused to function. Refused to create.

Bloody hell.

Thatcher's grumbling panic was interrupted by a familiar voice. "Thatcher, my good man! Is that you, lost in the wilderness of your thoughts?"

Startled, Thatcher turned to see his actor friend, Edward Waverly—a baron's throwaway spare, like him—approaching with a jovial grin on his face. Edward, a tall and dashing figure, had a charm that endeared him to both the theatre-going crowds and the ladies of London Society. Something he liked to boast about after too much ale.

Thatcher forced a smile, masking his inner turmoil. "Edward, you old rogue. Me? Lost? Not exactly, just...pondering."

Edward clapped him on the back heartily. "Ah, pondering! The curse of the creative mind. What's troubling you today, my friend? More pressing matters from the king, I presume?"

Thatcher nodded, the weight of the royal request heavy on his shoulders. "Aye, Edward. The king seeks another play, and

I'm afraid my well of inspiration has run dry."

Edward raised an eyebrow, concern in his eyes. "You jest, surely. You're Thatcher Goodrich, the greatest playwright in all of England! The king's favorite, no less."

Thatcher sighed, a bitter smile tugging at his lips. "It seems even the king's favorite can't escape the grip of writer's block. Please, tell no one of this."

"Of course not! You know you can rely on me to keep your confidence."

They strolled along the autumn path, engaged in animated conversation about the theatre, its fickle audience, and the ever-elusive muse. Thatcher kept his writer's block a closely guarded secret from the world, not wanting to burden anyone with his troubles. But this was Edward, one of his oldest and most trusted chums. And, well, it felt good to finally air the vile truth.

After a while, Edward bade him farewell, promising to meet for drinks at their favorite tavern later in the evening. As he watched his friend's retreating figure, Thatcher was once again alone with his thoughts. So he continued his aimless wandering through the park, the weight of his predicament pressing down on him like a leaden curtain. The king's request loomed over him, a daunting challenge he couldn't ignore.

Thatcher's brooding footsteps carried him farther into the park's depths. The dense canopy of trees cast elongated shadows across his path, adding to the melancholy that clung to him like a persistent specter. His hands remained buried deep within the pockets of his greatcoat, a futile attempt to shield himself from the chill of both the weather and his own rampant insecurities. He wandered beneath the centuries-old oaks, their gnarled branches intertwined like secrets whispered among confidants. The crisp scent of damp earth mingled with the faint fragrance of autumn flowers, offering a rare moment of respite from his relentless inner turmoil.

As he followed a winding trail, his thoughts circled back to the enigmatic King William and his unquenchable thirst for entertainment. Thatcher had once basked in the monarch's favor, reveling in the royal accolades and financial rewards. But now, the inkwell of inspiration had run dry, and a suffocating dread clung to his heart. He prided himself on his ability to craft captivating stories, to breathe life into characters that lingered in the hearts and minds of those who witnessed his plays. But the blank pages before him had become his greatest adversaries, mocking him with their emptiness.

His internal monologue grew louder, filled with self-doubt and frustration, screaming at him, *You're a fool, Thatcher! A fraud. They'll see through your charade. Your name will be forever tarnished.*

Lost in his thoughts, Thatcher failed to notice the hidden wonders of the park—rabbits darting among the bushes, birds singing their melodies, and the gentle trickle of a nearby stream that fed into the great Serpentine. It was a place untouched by the pretensions of London Society, where nature held court in all its untamed glory. As he continued his solitary journey, his restless mind seemed to guide him toward a curious discovery. Ahead to his right, nestled beneath a twisted thicket of brambles, half buried in a bed of vibrant, flowering bushes, lay a forgotten treasure—a journal. The once-bright red cover was now stained and tattered, and its pages bore the wear and tear of time. "What's this?" he murmured. *Intriguing.*

Thatcher bent down to retrieve the forlorn journal, its presence in this secluded spot a mystery he couldn't unravel. As he opened its fragile pages, his eyes widened in surprise, and a spark of intrigue ignited within him. The journal was filled with meticulous notes, character sketches, and even a reimagined ending for his *own* third act from his last play! "Oh, what delightful curiousness!"

His initial intrigue grew into fascination as he continued to leaf through the journal's contents. The elegant handwriting and creative insights hinted at a talent that rivaled his own. Yet there was no name to identify the journal's owner, no clues to the mysterious playwright behind these pages. Thatcher's heart quickened as he realized the true significance of his find. Here, in his hands, lay the work of an undiscovered genius—an artist whose brilliance had remained hidden from the world.

And in the midst of his creative despair, the discovery of this journal was a lifeline, a glimmer of hope that reignited the fires of inspiration within him.

With each page he turned, the gravity of his situation began to shift. The king's request no longer loomed as an insurmountable obstacle; instead, it became a canvas upon which he could paint the words of an unknown genius. A daring idea began to take root in his mind—a daring act that would forever change the course of his life. Thatcher knew he couldn't let this opportunity slip through his fingers. With determination burning in his moody eyes, he made a decision—to claim the journal as his own and present its contents as his latest masterpiece. The world would marvel at his newfound brilliance, unaware of the mysterious muse who had unknowingly breathed life into his words.

As he carefully stashed the journal within the folds of his greatcoat, Thatcher felt a renewed sense of eagerness and hope coursing through him. Quickly, he retraced his steps, making his way back to the heart of London. He left the enchanting tranquility of Hyde Park behind, the stolen journal safely tucked away in his coat, its presence igniting a simmering excitement within him. He couldn't help but wonder about the enigmatic writer whose words breathed new life into his stagnant creativity.

Thatcher strode through the bustling streets of London, the cacophony of the city enveloping him once more. Carriages clattered by, their wheels kicking up mud from the rain-soaked streets. The rhythmic din of horse hooves echoed through the narrow thoroughfares, a stark contrast to the serene solitude of the park he'd left behind. His destination was Rhodes Theatre, a hallowed stage where his greatest triumphs had been realized. There, the playwrights and actors of London congregated to bring stories to life, to entertain the masses and leave them spellbound in the dimly lit auditorium.

Once inside the theatre, he was greeted by the familiar scent of aged wood and the hushed whispers of actors and stagehands going about their preparations. The electric energy that permeated the air was a reminder of the magic that unfolded within these walls every night. Magic he, as the resident playwright, helped create.

Thatcher's thoughts turned to the journal tucked securely within his coat. The pages brimmed with inspiration, a veritable treasure trove of creativity that would surely captivate London's theatre-goers. He couldn't afford to let this opportunity slip away, not when his reputation and livelihood were at stake.

A quick nip of guilty conscience bit him, and he glanced toward the ornately carved ceiling of the theatre. "Surely you understand?' he implored, believing anyone in his position would fault him not at all for what he was about to do. "Of course you do," he decided, snapping to attention once more.

With resolute determination, he ascended the narrow staircase that led to his modest office. He closed the door behind him, ensuring his secret remained hidden from prying eyes. The flickering candlelight cast dancing shadows across the room, a fitting backdrop for the clandestine act he was about to undertake. Carefully, Thatcher retrieved the journal from his coat and placed it on his cluttered desk. He traced the faded ink on its pages, absorbing the words and ideas that had the power to reignite his career. He couldn't help but marvel at the genius that had remained concealed for far too long. The play—the one that bore no author's name—was a tale filled with wit, passion, and an undeniable flair for the dramatic. Each line sang with a lyrical quality that resonated deeply with him, and he couldn't deny the impact it would have on an audience.

A sense of urgency washed over Thatcher as he considered. The play was a masterpiece in its own right, a work of art that deserved to be seen and celebrated. But its lack of attribution presented a dilemma. How could he present it to the world without revealing its true source?

His mind whirled with possibilities and risks. He knew the consequences of plagiarism were severe, and he had no intention of tarnishing his reputation further. However, he also recognized the value of this hidden gem and the potential it held to save his career. With a mixture of guilt and determination, he decided on a course of action. He would present the play as his own, offering a masterful performance on the stage to match its brilliance on paper. It was a daring act, one that carried the weight of deceit, but in the ruthless world of theatre, where ambition reigned supreme, he couldn't afford to let this opportunity pass. This truth he knew all too well. Too personally.

Thatcher glanced at the ornate mirror that adorned his office wall, his reflection a portrait of contemplation. He knew he was venturing into uncharted territory, risking not only his reputation but also his sense of integrity. Yet the allure of the stage, the adoration of the audience, and the tantalizing promise of redemption were too potent to resist. As was not defaulting on King William's request. Could he face imprisonment for failure to deliver a play?

He shuddered. *That* he wished never to discover.

With the stolen journal as his secret muse, Thatcher prepared to embark on a journey that would challenge the very essence of his artistry. He would bring the hidden play to life, captivating audiences and critics alike.

Little did he know that this decision would set in motion a series of events that would forever alter the course of his life, leading him down a path of unforeseen passion, desire, and entangled destinies.

Thatcher's mind continued to race as he contemplated the audacious plan he had devised. It was a risky gambit, one that could either resurrect his fading career or send him plummeting into the abyss of theatrical infamy.

He would need to immerse himself fully in the journal's contents, adapting the enigmatic playwright's words to the stage.

It would be a formidable challenge, one that demanded every ounce of his creative prowess and cunning.

The office door creaked open, and Thatcher's heart skipped a beat. He hastily closed the journal, concealing his secret, and turned to face the intruder.

"Thatcher, you look positively stricken," said Arthur Weston, a Rhodes actor and friend.

Thatcher managed a forced smile. "Ah, Arthur, you always have impeccable timing."

Arthur chuckled. "I see you've been huddled away in your den of creativity again. What hidden gems are you conjuring up this time?"

Thatcher's mind raced for a suitable diversion. "Just the usual musings. You know how it is—the life of a playwright is fraught with inspiration and despair in equal measure."

Arthur leaned against the doorframe, his eyes twinkling with mischief. "Inspiration and despair? I must say, Thatcher, you've always had a flair for the dramatic, even in your conversations. It's a quality I've always admired."

Thatcher couldn't help but smirk. Arthur had an uncanny ability to lighten even the heaviest of moods. "I suppose I'm living up to my profession, then. Speaking of which, how fares our esteemed troupe?"

Arthur's expression shifted to a more serious one. "The actors are eager, as always, to bring your words to life, my friend. But I've noticed a shadow looming over you recently. Is there something you're not telling me?"

Thatcher hesitated, torn between the desire to confide in his friend like he had with Edward, and the fear of revealing his clandestine actions. "It's nothing. Just a bout of struggling inspiration, nothing more."

Arthur raised an eyebrow, his perceptive gaze drilling into Thatcher's façade. "Struggling inspiration, you say? That's not like you, old chap. You've always been a wellspring of creativity, even in the face of adversity."

Thatcher averted his eyes, unable to meet Arthur's probing stare. "We all have our moments of weakness. I assure you, it's merely a temporary setback."

Arthur seemed satisfied with his explanation, though a trace of concern lingered in his blunt features. "Very well. You know I'm here if you ever need to share your burdens."

Thatcher forced a reassuring smile. "I appreciate that. Now, tell me, have you any plans for the evening? A night of revelry, perhaps?"

Arthur's face lit up with enthusiasm. "Indeed! I've heard whispers of a new tavern in Covent Garden, the Meadowlark. They say it's a haven for artists and free spirits. Care to join me for a pint or two?"

Thatcher considered the invitation. A night of diversion might help him temporarily set aside his moral quandary. "Why not? A change of scenery might be just what I need."

⇥⟫⟪⇤

AS THEY MADE their way to the bustling streets of London, Thatcher couldn't help but feel a twinge of guilt. He was about to embark on a journey that would blur the lines between inspiration and deception, all while the stolen journal weighed heavily on his conscience. He pushed it aside and took in a steadying breath. One did what one had to do. Hadn't his old man always yelled those exact words when he'd used his fists in a drunken rage, saying it was the only way to make his wayward spawns mind?

Christ, he didn't need to think about that now.

Stop it.

The evening air in Covent Garden was alive with the vibrant energy of the city's nightlife. Lanterns hung from the eaves of taverns, casting a warm, inviting glow onto cobblestone streets. Laughter and music spilled out from the bustling establishments, promising an escape from the cares of the world. Thatcher found himself with Arthur at the entrance of the Meadowlark Tavern, drawn in by the lively atmosphere and the promise of good company. As they stepped inside, they were greeted by the aroma of hearty pub fare and the sounds of a fiddle playing a lively tune.

The tavern's interior was cozy and dimly lit, with wooden beams overhead and rough-hewn tables that bore the scars of countless tankards and merriment. A diverse crowd of patrons filled the space, from actors in flamboyant costumes to writers hunched over their manuscripts, their quills poised in anticipation.

They settled at a corner table, Thatcher appreciating the relative privacy it offered. Arthur signaled for the barmaid, a buxom redhead with a mischievous twinkle in her eye, and ordered a round of ale. "And keep 'em coming, will ya?" He turned his brown gaze on Thatcher. "So, Goodrich," Arthur began, his voice barely audible over the tavern's din, "tell me more about this damnable lack of inspiration that's been plaguing you."

Thatcher sighed, his earlier elation over the unsigned play waning. He couldn't escape the weight of his predicament, even in the midst of revelry. "It's as if the muse has temporarily abandoned me. Nothing life-threatening." Though it could be, if he didn't deliver a new play for the king.

Arthur nodded sympathetically. "A writer without his words is like an actor without an audience. Perhaps you need a change of scenery to rekindle your creativity and get that inspiration flowing again."

Thatcher couldn't help but chuckle at his friend's attempt to lift his spirits. "A change of scenery is precisely what I sought tonight." He realized he shouldn't share more, so he added with a fake smile, "It's already working. Those words tumbling around in my head like stones in a river."

In truth, the specter of that blank page haunted him.

Their conversation was interrupted by the raucous arrival of a group of actors, their voices raised in jovial camaraderie.

Among them was Sarah, a vivacious ensemble actress with fiery red hair and an infectious laugh. She swept Arthur into an enthusiastic embrace, her cheeks flushed with merriment. "Arthur, darling!" she exclaimed, planting a kiss on his cheek. "You're just in time. Join us for a drink!"

"Do you mind?" Arthur asked, clearly wishing to join the others.

"Bollocks with you and be gone," Thatcher growled, and waved him off with a grin. "Imbibe and make merry."

With that, Arthur melted into the group. Thatcher observed the lively scene with a mixture of envy and detachment. While he appreciated the camaraderie of the thespians, he couldn't shake the feeling of being an outsider, burdened by his secret. Well, *secrets*. The writer's block and the mystery journal of brilliance.

As the night wore on, Thatcher found himself lost in contemplation, his mind returning to the stolen journal hidden away in his room. He knew he couldn't delay any longer; he had a duty to the king and a desperate need to regain his creative spark. The time had come to pull up his bootstraps and get it done.

Finally, with a sense of resolve, he excused himself from the night's revelry, leaving Arthur and the actors to their merriment. He walked the dimly lit streets of Covent Garden, the weight of his decision settling upon him. Arriving back at his townhouse, he ascended the stairs to his private study, where his own journal lay hidden beneath a stack of manuscripts. With a sense of trepidation, he retrieved it and settled into his writing desk, quill in hand.

The words flowed from his pen as if they had been waiting for release, guided by the unseen hand of destiny. The stolen words of the enigmatic playwright played in his mind and merged with his own ideas. Hours turned into the early morning as Thatcher worked tirelessly, his determination unwavering. By the time the first light of dawn filtered through his study window, he had crafted the framework of a new play, one that bore the marks of his genius and the hidden contributions of a mysterious muse.

As he gazed at the completed pages before him, exhaustion

and exhilaration washing over him in equal measure, he couldn't deny the thrill of creation. It was a feeling he had longed for, one that had eluded him for too long.

And he had one unidentified writer to thank.

CHAPTER THREE

L OTTIE STOOD BEFORE her full-length mirror, her reflection cast in the soft glow of candlelight. Her gown, a rich sapphire silk adorned with delicate lace, clung to her tall, statuesque figure, accentuating her graceful presence. Her quiet blue eyes and long, wheat-colored hair added to her quiet beauty, but she was the most unremarkable of the three Castlebury sisters. Or so her mother always claimed.

She should have felt elated. After all, it was a night at the theatre—a lavish event filled with music, laughter, and drama. But Lottie's heart was heavy with an unsettling absence. Her fingers trembled as she reached for her evening bag, a delicate creation made of satin and lace. She carried it with her everywhere, and tonight was no exception. Yet, as her gloved hand brushed against the bag, she felt a sudden chill of dread as her mind reeled back to earlier in Hyde Park.

Her gaze flew to her old bag. The satchel's once-pristine seam had given way, leaving a frayed gap at the bottom. Lottie's breath caught in her throat as she saw the empty space where her precious journal should have rested, reminding her. Panic welled up inside her once more as she searched the room, her frantic gaze darting from one piece of furniture to another.

"Where is it?" she muttered, her voice stricken with anxiety. She couldn't afford to lose that journal—it held not only her personal thoughts and ideas but also her most cherished creations, the plays she had penned in secret! Oh, she had looked everywhere between Tipton House and the park. It *had* to be in her chambers somewhere. For it was clearly nowhere else on God's green earth!

Why, yesterday afternoon she'd even sent Bailey, the youngest footman, to comb the neighborhood. He'd found nothing.

"Come on, come on, where are you?"

"Lottie, dear, are you all right?" her mother called suddenly from the adjoining room.

Taking a deep breath to compose herself, Lottie lied, "I'm fine, Mother. Just a moment of forgetfulness." It was a blatant falsity, one she hoped her mother wouldn't see through.

The candlelight in the bedchamber cast dancing shadows on the walls as she stood in the center of the room and listened as her mother dismissed her, believing her falsehood.

Her thoughts were consumed by a single, maddening question: where was her journal?

Lottie had carried that weathered journal with her everywhere, a constant companion through the ups and downs of her life. Losing it was unthinkable!

She searched the room meticulously, overturning cushions, rifling through drawers, and even peering under the bed. But the journal remained elusive, like a phantom that refused to be found.

"Miss Lottie, is there something I can help you with?" her maid, Martha, asked tentatively as she entered the room. She had been with the Castlebury family for years and had a keen sense for when something was amiss.

Lottie turned to Martha, her eyes wide with panic. "My journal—I can't find it anywhere. I had it with me in my bag until I noticed it missing at the park yesterday. I've searched all over!"

Martha's expression mirrored Lottie's concern. "Your journal, miss? The one you keep your writings in?"

Lottie nodded vigorously, her heart racing. "Yes, that's the one. I can't go on without it. It's...everything to me."

Her maid stepped closer, her age-lined face filled with empathy. "We'll find it, miss. Let's search together. Where was the last place you remember having it?"

Lottie's mind raced, trying to recall the moments leading up to her frantic search. "I had it on my writing desk," she replied, her voice trembling. "I was reviewing some notes before I started getting dressed...then I went downstairs and argued with those blockheads...then I walked to the park and home again..."

"Did you take it on the walk with you?"

"I believe so. I mean, I think so?" Lottie thought on it a moment. "I was in a snit when I left, grabbing my bag in a huff. So perhaps I didn't take it...?" Her gaze fell to her desk.

The two of them hurried to the writing desk, where Lottie had spent countless hours crafting her stories. It was a place of solace and inspiration, and the journal had been a constant presence there. But as they arrived at the desk, it was painfully clear that the journal was missing. Lottie felt a deep sense of loss, as if a part of her had been torn away.

"Miss, could it have fallen somewhere?" Martha asked gently, her eyes scanning the room.

Lottie bit her lip, considering the possibility. "Perhaps," she replied, her voice tinged with desperation. "But I've looked everywhere in this room. I've looked all over Hyde Park and Mayfair. I've retraced my steps. It's as if it disappeared."

Martha didn't respond immediately. Instead, she began to search the room anew, her experienced eyes spotting details that Lottie might have missed. As they combed through the bedchamber together, Martha's voice offered a reassuring presence. "We'll find it, Miss Lottie," she said, determination in her voice. "I'll have the other servants help in the search. It couldn't have gone far."

Lottie nodded, her gratitude for Martha's support palpable. Losing her journal felt like losing a piece of herself.

As they continued their search, Lottie couldn't help but worry about the consequences of its disappearance. Her thoughts were filled with the fear that someone might discover her secret passion for playwriting, a pursuit deemed improper for a lady of her station. But more than that, she felt a profound sense of loss, as if her very own identity was slipping through her fingers. Someone out there could be reading her *most personal thoughts.*

Good God, no.

"What if someone identifies it as mine?" she worried aloud.

Martha's eyes widened in understanding. "Oh my, I'm sure it will turn up. Perhaps you left it in the drawing room or the library."

"Oh, Martha, it's everything to me. I can't bear the thought of someone finding it and reading my ideas."

Martha hurried to her mistress's side and placed a comforting hand on her arm. "We'll retrace your steps. We'll go back and search Hyde Park if we must. We'll find your journal."

Lottie's eyes welled up with tears, and she gave a grateful nod. "Thank you, Martha. I don't know what I would do without you."

With determination, Lottie and Martha left her bedchamber. They retraced Lottie's steps through the grand halls of Tipton House, checking every room and nook she had passed through yesterday. Lottie's agitation only grew with each empty-handed search. "I'm certain I had it with me when I left the drawing room," she muttered as they entered the opulent sitting area adorned with gilded furniture and rich tapestries. "I was reading through my notes, going over the dialogue for the new play, when Rainville and Crawford came in and we began arguing."

Martha scanned the room and then moved toward a large, plush armchair. "Perhaps you left it here."

Lottie's heart raced as she rushed over to the chair and began frantically searching its cushions and crevices. Her fingers brushed against the soft fabric, but there was no sign of her beloved journal. "Nothing," she said, her voice quivering with frustration. "It's not here."

"We won't give up. Let's retrace your steps from the moment you left this room." They continued their search throughout

Tipton House. Lottie's anxious energy filled every room they entered, but the journal remained elusive.

As they descended the grand staircase, Lottie's mother, Lady Castlebury, appeared at the bottom, her expression a mixture of concern and curiosity. She was an elegant and poised woman, her silver-threaded red hair perfectly coiffed, and her eyes filled with maternal worry. "Lottie, dear, what is the matter?" she asked.

Lottie took a deep breath, trying to calm herself. "Mother, I've lost my journal—the one where I write all my plays. I can't find it anywhere."

Lady Castlebury's eyes softened with sympathy, and she moved closer to her daughter. "Oh dear. We'll help you look for it. It must be here somewhere."

Lottie appreciated her mother's support but couldn't help feeling a sense of urgency. The theatre awaited them all, and she couldn't bear the thought of facing the stage without her precious journal to take notes in. The clock on the wall chimed, a reminder that time slipped away.

Martha suggested they check the library once more, and Lottie reluctantly agreed. As they entered the library, Lottie's gaze fell on the large oak desk where she often sat. Her heart skipped a beat, and she rushed over to it.

Nothing.

Despite their exhaustive search, the journal remained elusive. Lottie's heart sank as the minutes ticked away, and the realization set in that she would have to leave for the Rhodes Theatre without it. She looked at the clock on the wall. Time had run out.

Martha shared in Lottie's distress. "We've searched every inch of the house. It's nowhere to be found. What will you do?"

Lottie's jaw clenched with determination. She couldn't delay any longer. "I'll have to go without it. I can't keep the family waiting any longer. But we will continue searching as soon as I return."

But as Lottie rejoined her family in the drawing room, she couldn't shake the unease gnawing at her. She was surrounded by her loved ones—her mother, her sisters Carenza and Nora, her brothers-in-law Rainville and Damon, her brother Crawford, and his wife Sadie—but a sense of disquiet clung to her. Their chatter, filled with anticipation for the evening's performance at Rhodes Theatre, felt distant and insignificant as Lottie's mind raced. She needed her journal, her lifeline to the world of storytelling and creativity. Without it, she felt adrift, unmoored.

As the family prepared to leave, Lottie made a final, desperate search of her bedchamber. But the journal remained elusive, as if it had vanished into thin air. She forced a smile, hoping to conceal her anxiety from her family, and followed them out of the house.

A curse on anyone who touched her precious journal.

⇶⟫⟪⟪

RHODES THEATRE, AN opulent venue in the heart of London, was bathed in a warm glow as the gas lamps lining the entrance illuminated the night. The Castlebury family arrived in style, greeted by the theatre's staff, who were well acquainted with their status as patrons—and family to the theatre's owner, the Duke of Somerton.

Inside the theatre, Lottie took her seat with her family in the private box, her nerves on edge. She had attended countless performances here, but tonight was different. Tonight, she had no journal.

As the curtains rose, Lottie's heart pounded in her chest, her love for the theatre momentarily overriding her worry. The play that unfolded before her eyes was a masterpiece—a brilliant tapestry of wit, drama, and romance. It held her utterly transfixed.

It was a work of art—and it was *hers*. Every line, every character, every nuance, was unmistakably her creation. *Hers*. Lady Lottie Castlebury's. "What in the bloody hell?" she mumbled, dumbfounded.

Her eyes widened in shock as she watched the actors breathe

life into the words she had penned in her journal. The scenes unfolded with an eerie familiarity, as if the characters had leaped from the pages of her imagination and onto the stage. All of it— all that lovely, extraordinary creation—was hers.

She couldn't believe it.

How?

Why?

Oh shite, my journal, she thought with a sinking, greasy feeling. It had to be her from her journal. Blast it, that was her missing play!

Who could have done this?

The words played round and round in her mind as the play continued, and she watched until the perfect third act ending.

Who?

Why?

Then *he* appeared. Thatcher Goodrich, the renowned playwright, stepped forward to take his bow. The audience erupted in applause, and King William himself declared Goodrich the finest playwright in all of England, a contemporary of Shakespeare. And it hit her.

Thatcher bloody Goodrich. That was who.

Thief.

Thief!

Lottie seethed with anger as she watched Goodrich bask in the adulation. Adulation that should have been hers. He'd stolen her play, claimed her genius as his own—and now he reveled in the praise of the aristocracy and the monarch himself! It was an affront, a betrayal she could not bear. "How dare he?" she seethed between her teeth, digging her nails into her palms.

As the applause continued, Lottie's vision narrowed to a burning point of fury. The stolen words of her play echoed in her mind. She vowed then that she would confront Goodrich, expose him for the fraud he was, and reclaim her rightful place as the true playwright.

It was her hard work, damn it.

CHAPTER FOUR

THE BACKSTAGE AREA hummed with post-performance elation and frenetic energy. Actors bustled about, their voices carrying snippets of hushed conversations, while others divested themselves of their extravagant costumes, chatting and reliving the evening's performance. The room was ripe with the fragrance of greasepaint and the distant echoes of the orchestra still playing their instruments, bidding farewell to the attendees with a graceful ode to Handel.

Amid the normal post-play chaos, Thatcher stood like a solitary figure in the middle of a storm. His dark, unruly hair framed his brooding countenance, and his eyes, the color of a riotous sea, were fixed intently on the wooden dressing table before him. The table was cluttered with scattered scripts, half-empty inkwells, and an assortment of quills, each waiting to etch his genius onto parchment.

His attire was a somber ensemble of a dark velvet coat and waistcoat to match his mood, he belatedly noted with some irony, as his fingers danced lightly across a crumpled page, attempting to coax inspiration from the depths of his mind. He was a man driven by the relentless pursuit of his art, an artist who had elevated the London stage to new heights through sheer determination to succeed.

Tonight, he had succeeded in excess.

The atmosphere backstage shifted abruptly, like a tempest

gale sweeping through the room, extinguishing the frenzied voices and quelling the restless energy. Thatcher's head snapped up, his eyes widening in a mixture of awe and disbelief.

A lady had arrived.

Thatcher's breath caught in his throat as he beheld the vision before him.

"Lady Carlotta Castlebury," he heard someone whisper from behind, sounding awestruck.

With her hair cascading in golden waves down her tall and statuesque form, she moved with a regal poise that demanded recognition. His attention. And oh, did she possess it.

As he stupidly stared on, her azure eyes blazed with an inner fire, and her lips, soft and beguiling, thinned and set in a determined line. She was a force of nature, this woman. Her entrance sent ripples through the backstage milieu. Actors paused in their preparations, stagehands exchanged knowing glances, and the air itself seemed to quiver with sudden anticipation. The theatre was no stranger to drama, but this unexpected intrusion promised a spectacle of an entirely different kind. Why, she practically shot sparks!

Hot, beguiling, luminous sparks.

Oh, shut up, you bloody cockled poet. Sometimes he annoyed the shite out of himself. Nobody wanted his gushing linguistic nonsense. Not even him.

As Lady Lottie's gaze locked on to Thatcher, a charged silence enveloped the room. He felt an undeniable magnetic pull, a tumultuous mixture of attraction and apprehension, leaving him momentarily breathless. "Lady Lottie," he murmured, his voice tinged with a blend of awe and disbelief as their worlds collided.

He felt it. The shift. The tilt. The clicking of cogs into place.

Nothing would be the same.

Thatcher just knew it.

Ah, hell.

Lady Lottie's blue eyes blazed with a fury rivaling the most fearsome of storms as she confronted him amidst the backstage chaos. Her presence seemed to suck the air from the room, leaving his chest tight and wheezing. He prided himself on his poise and eloquence, but found himself struggling to maintain his composure. Shifting his weight uneasily, he darted his eyes about restlessly as he searched for the right words to counter her coming (and utterly true) accusations.

"What on earth are you doing here, Lady Lottie?" he finally managed to say, though his voice lacked the confident resonance that typically accompanied his words.

Her lips curled into a sneer, and her gaze bored into him like she was a hawk zeroing in on its prey. "I should think it's quite evident, Mr. Goodrich. I've come to confront the thief who stole my play!"

Thatcher's brows knitted together, and he glanced around, making sure none of the actors or crew members were eavesdropping on their heated exchange, his stomach clenching at her words. Everyone seemed quite focused on their tasks. Which, of course, meant they were listening. "Lower your voice, Lady Lottie. We're in the midst of cleaning up after the performance, and these esteemed talents require silence as they settle themselves after such exertion and effort."

Lottie clenched her fists at her sides, her frustration palpable. "I don't care about your precious silence, Mr. Goodrich. I care about the play you shamelessly claimed as your own just now!"

He sighed, trying to regain some semblance of composure. "Lady Lottie, I assure you, I have no idea what you're talking about." Though he did. He knew *exactly* what she was talking about.

This lady was the owner of the journal.

The playwright was a lady.

This lady.

Thatcher's palms went damp, and he swallowed hard. Such brilliant talent inside her mind! A mind wrapped in the most alluring package. What was he to do?

"Don't play the innocent with me, sir. The play you performed tonight, the one you proudly declared as your creation, is *mine.*" The lady's voice dripped with disdain.

Thatcher widened his eyes in feigned surprise, and he was momentarily at a loss for words. "That's preposterous. I wrote this play myself."

He watched her anger flare in fascination, noting the beautiful flush it brought to her skin, and she took an aggressive step closer to him. "You must think me a fool, Mr. Goodrich. I recognize my own words, my own characters. I even recognized my own quotes in some of the revisions."

Thatcher ran a hand through his hair. "This is absurd, Lady Lottie. I can't explain how you might believe such a thing, but I can assure you that this play is entirely my own work."

He had to figure a way out of this—and fast.

⋙⋘

"NOW, YOU HOLD it right there," Mr. Goodrich began.

"No, *you* hold it," Lottie cut in, uncaring that their heated exchange had not gone unnoticed, and the actors and crew nearby had fallen into a hushed silence, casting furtive glances at the dramatic confrontation unfolding before them.

Lottie's voice quivered with a mixture of anger and desperation as she stared down the unbelievable man. "I have no reason to lie, Mr. Goodrich. That play is my creation, and you've stolen it!"

Thatcher's eyes flickered with a range of emotions—defiance, guilt, and a hint of vulnerability. He leaned in closer, his voice a low, intense murmur. "Lady Lottie, even if what you say is true, what proof do you have? You're a woman. How can you convince anyone that you're the true author of this play?"

Lottie met his gaze, her resolve unyielding, fury a hot ball in her stomach. "I'll find a way, Mr. Goodrich. I'll fight to reclaim what's rightfully mine. And you, sir, will answer for your theft."

As their confrontation reached its peak, the backstage area at Rhodes Theatre crackled with tension. Lottie's cheeks flushed with righteous anger. Her blue eyes, usually so serene, blazed with intensity. "You thief!" she accused. "You stole my play, and you dare to take credit for it! The arrogance! How *dare* you?"

Thatcher clenched his jaw. "I did no such thing, Lady Lottie. I am an esteemed playwright. Why would I need to steal your work?"

"Oh, I don't know, perhaps because your own well of creativity has run dry?"

Thatcher went very pale. "You know nothing," he finally snapped.

Exchanging barbs and accusations, they didn't hear Rainville, the Duke of Somerton and the theatre's owner, enter the scene, his imposing presence commanding attention. He surveyed the situation with a raised bronzed eyebrow, a master of control and diplomacy. "Lady Lottie, Mr. Goodrich, I must insist on decorum backstage," he declared, his voice a low rumble that brooked no argument. "We've guests still in attendance."

Lottie shot a glare at Thatcher before turning her attention to Rainville. "Look, I beg your pardon, but this man has stolen my play. I cannot stand idly by while he reaps the rewards of my hard labor!"

Thatcher's mouth twisted into a smirk. "*Your* play, Lady Lottie? I have never seen any evidence of your involvement in this production."

"It is from my missing journal," she practically growled, her jaw clenched tight enough to crack.

Rainville's expression remained impassive as he listened to their conflicting claims. "I suggest we address this matter calmly and rationally, rather than resorting to a public spectacle. The reputation of Rhodes Theatre is at stake."

Lottie took a deep breath, her anger simmering beneath the surface. "Very well, Duke. But mark my words, Mr. Goodrich, I will prove your theft."

The bloody thief met her challenge with a defiant glint in his unfairly gorgeous, smoke-colored eyes. "I welcome any investigation, Lady Lottie. The truth will prevail."

Their confrontation may have been temporarily defused, but the tension lingered between them, like a smoldering ember. Lottie's voice, though still seething with anger, took on a measured tone. "Mr. Goodrich, you may have fooled the world, but you haven't fooled me. I recognized my own words, my own ideas, on that stage."

His unreadable gaze bored into hers, his voice low and challenging. "And how, Lady Lottie, do you explain the fact that you've never shared your play with anyone? No one in the theatre knew of its existence."

"Because I guard my work fiercely, fearing that someone might steal it. Yet, somehow, you managed to do just that."

Rainville remained a silent, watchful presence. His keen eyes darted between the two of them, adversaries of the first order. Clearly he was assessing the situation. For he knew that the reputation of Rhodes Theatre was at stake, and he couldn't afford a scandal. Not with Nora's own scandal so recent in the past.

"Lottie," he finally interjected, "I understand your concerns, but let us not jump to conclusions. Accusations alone do not constitute proof."

Lottie's cheeks flushed with a mixture of frustration and indignation. Oh, she *had* proof. How about she quote every damned line from memory? "I have been working on that play for months. I know every word, every nuance. I assure you, that play on the stage is mine."

Thatcher's lips curled into a wry smile. "Then, Lady Lottie, you must be an exceptionally talented playwright to have created a work that so closely resembles my own style."

"I won't stand for this, Mr. Goodrich! I will find the evidence to prove your theft."

He met her challenge with an easy smile. "Feel free to try, Lady Lottie. But I assure you, the truth is on my side."

Rainville, ever the diplomat, spoke with authority. "This matter will be addressed privately. For now, we have an encore performance to deliver. Lady Lottie, Mr. Goodrich, I trust that you can set aside your differences for the sake of the theatre."

Lottie's spine cracked with stiffness, but she nodded in reluctant agreement. Thatcher, too, gave a curt nod. Rainville's piercing gold gaze swept over the assembled actors and crew members, effectively silencing the whispers that had spread like wildfire in the wake of Lottie's confrontation of their esteemed playwright.

Thatcher stood there in his bloody dark, brooding clothes, his dark gray eyes glinting with defiance. Fortunately for him, he appeared to have the wisdom not to challenge the duke's authority. After all, Rainville was not just the theatre owner; he was a peer of the realm, and his word was law in his domain.

Lottie, though visibly seething, was equally aware of the situation's delicacy. She had always admired Rainville for his astute management of the theatre, and she knew that this was not the time or place for a prolonged argument. As much as she wanted it to be.

"Ladies and gentlemen, actors and stagehands, we put on a grand performance," Rainville boomed. "The success of this play is paramount for Rhodes, and I will not tolerate any further disruptions that may tarnish our reputation. Now, get out there with that encore."

A collective nod of understanding rippled through the room. The actors and crew members knew better than to defy the duke's wishes, especially on an opening night.

But Rainville wasn't finished. With a discerning look, he turned his gaze back to them. "Lady Lottie, Mr. Goodrich, I trust you both understand the gravity of your roles this night. The spotlight is on Rhodes, and the eyes of London's theatre elite are upon us. Stop your squabbling."

Lottie swallowed her pride and replied with forced civility, "Of course, Your Grace. The show must go on."

Thatcher, clearly a master of masking his true emotions, offered a polite nod of agreement. "Indeed, Your Grace. We shall not allow personal matters to overshadow the encore performance."

Rainville's stern countenance softened slightly. "Very well, then. Let us proceed with the final preparations. And remember, we are a family here at Rhodes Theatre. We support one another, even in moments of disagreement." With that, the duke exited the backstage area, leaving behind a trail of lingering tension and unresolved issues. Lottie exchanged one last, heated glance with Thatcher before she too turned her attention to the upcoming encore, curious despite herself. That, she hadn't written.

The backstage chaos resumed, albeit with a subtle undercurrent of curiosity about the lingering conflict. Actors hurriedly reapplied makeup, adjusted costumes, and ran through their lines. Crew members scurried about, ensuring that the set was in perfect order.

Thatcher, despite his awfulness, was a consummate professional. In fact, he was one hell of an actor himself.

He pretended she didn't exist at all.

When all was finally finished, Rainville reappeared. "Follow me now."

Lottie didn't need to be told twice.

CHAPTER FIVE

R AINVILLE TOOK LONG strides, leading the way to his office within the theatre. Thatcher followed, his expression dark. He knew he was in trouble, but his stubbornness wouldn't allow him to admit it.

As they entered the lavishly decorated office, Lady Lottie's frustration boiled over. "You shameless thief!" she hissed at Thatcher, not caring that they were in the presence of a nobleman.

Thatcher scoffed, a sarcastic grin tugging at his lips. "Thief? My dear Lady Lottie, I assure you, I've never stolen anything in my life."

Lottie's cheeks flushed with righteous anger as she confronted him again. Like a fox on a rabbit's scent. "You thief!" she accused once again, her voice trembling with emotion. "You stole my play, and now you dare to continue lying about it!"

Thatcher felt a twinge of guilt, but it was quickly overridden by his stubborn determination, and his desperate need to never live as his father did—as his father made his children live. He clenched his jaw. "I did no such thing, Lady Lottie. I am perfectly capable of utilizing my own words. Why would I need to steal your work?"

"Oh, I don't know, *because you did.*"

The argument escalated in Rainville's fancy office, and the air was thick with tension. The duke stood tall and imposing behind his massive mahogany desk, his normally stoic face betraying hints of amusement and annoyance at their fiery exchange. "Enough!" he finally bellowed, his voice like thunder in the room. The force of his command silenced them both, and Thatcher turned his attention toward the duke. Rainville leaned against his desk, tapping his fingers rhythmically on its polished surface as he regarded the two squabbling artists. "I've had my fill of this senseless bickering. You're both talented individuals, and I'm not about to let your childish disputes disrupt the operations of my theatre."

Lottie opened her mouth to respond, but Rainville raised a quelling hand, silencing her. "Before you two can continue your delightful sparring, you ought to know that a new order has just arrived from the king."

Thatcher's eyes widened in surprise, and Lottie's anger must have been momentarily forgotten, because she too focused on Rainville with bright interest. "The king?" she asked.

Rainville nodded. "Indeed. King William has requested another new play, and this one he wants in two weeks."

Thatcher exchanged a shocked glance with Lady Lottie. Two weeks was an incredibly tight deadline for any playwright, even a seasoned professional! Christ, how could he manage two weeks when he couldn't finish a play right now even if he had two *years*? His face paled, and he knew Lady Lottie could see a hint of panic in his eyes. It was evident that the prospect of disappointing the king weighed heavily on him. That he could not hide, no matter how he tried.

A triumphant gleam flickered in Lady Lottie's eyes as she seized the opportunity to get back at him. "Two weeks? That doesn't leave much time for you to come up with something *original*, Mr. Goodrich. Does it?"

Thatcher shot her a withering glare but didn't rise to the bait. Instead, he turned his attention back to Rainville. "Your Grace, surely you don't expect me to complete a new play in such a short span! It's an impossible task."

"It's not my expectation, Mr. Goodrich. It's the king's command. He's the greatest admirer of your work."

Thatcher's confident façade crumbled like a sandcastle swept away by a rogue wave. His face turned a shade paler.

"Did you hear that, Mr. Goodrich?" Lady Lottie taunted him. "A new order from King William himself. I trust you're not too terrified to take on the task?"

Thatcher's response was nothing but a strained, tight-lipped smile, and he avoided her gaze. It was clear Lady Lottie knew that her relentless accusations and Rainville's announcement had shaken him to the core.

Then Rainville dropped another bombshell that left Thatcher stunned. "Lady Lottie," he said, "you shall be Mr. Goodrich's co-writer."

⭬⭬⭬⭰⭰⭰

THE DUKE'S WORDS hung in the air, and Lottie's jaw dropped. She had been prepared to stand her ground, to defend her work against Goodrich's theft, but she had never considered the possibility of working alongside the man who had betrayed her so callously! To ask such a thing of her!

Impossible.

Thatcher's eyes widened in disbelief, mirroring Lottie's shock. Her mind raced with conflicting emotions. Anger still burned hotly within her, but beneath it, a spark of determination flickered. She had always longed for her talent to be recognized, to have her name associated with her work, and this might be her chance! If she could turn this collaboration into an opportunity to showcase her skills, then perhaps the sacrifice would be worthwhile.

Thatcher, too, seemed to grasp the gravity of the situation. His shoulders tensed, and he cleared his throat. "Well, it appears we are to be co-writers," he muttered to her, his tone tinged with resignation.

Rainville nodded with satisfaction. "Excellent. Now that's settled, I expect nothing but the best from the two of you. The king has made his wishes clear, and I intend to deliver him a masterpiece."

With that, Rainville dismissed them, leaving Lottie alone with Thatcher in the office. The air between them was thick with unvoiced emotions, and as they made their way out, she couldn't shake the feeling that she had just embarked on an arduous journey, one that would test her patience, creativity, and perhaps even her sanity.

The theatre's backstage area buzzed with activity as they emerged from Rainville's office. Actors rushed past them, their voices a cacophony of excitement and satisfaction over a job well done. Lottie and Thatcher walked side by side through the labyrinthine corridors.

For a few moments, neither spoke, lost in their thoughts and grappling with the weight of the situation. Finally, it was Lottie who broke the silence, her voice low and filled with restrained anger. "I cannot believe I have to work with you," she muttered, her gaze fixed straight ahead. It wasn't fair.

Thatcher sighed, his breath almost visible in the chilly theatre air. "Believe me, Lady Lottie, the feeling is mutual."

Lottie shot him a sideways glance. "Think not for a moment that I will let you steal any more of my work."

His lips curved into a wry smile. "Rest assured, we will write this play together, and it will be as much your work as mine."

Lottie scoffed. "Do not mistake this for forgiveness, Mr. Goodrich. I will be watching you every step of the way."

Their footsteps echoed in the corridor as they continued to walk, their paths now inexorably linked by the king's command and Rainville's decree. They might be reluctant co-writers, but they knew that they had no choice but to collaborate, for the sake of their reputations and, in Lottie's case, for the chance to prove their worth in the world of theatre.

"I hope you're prepared to work, Mr. Goodrich, because I won't tolerate any of your procrastination or theatrics."

The playwright smirked. "Procrastination and theatrics? Lady Lottie, you wound me. I'll have you know I take my work very seriously."

Lottie's eyes rolled skyward. "Oh, please. I've heard all about your late-night carousing and your fondness for the taverns. You may be a playwright, but you're hardly the embodiment of dedication."

Thatcher chuckled, a low, throaty sound that sent a shiver down Lottie's spine, though she would never admit it. "Appearances can be deceiving. You'd be surprised at what one can achieve with a bit of midnight inspiration."

She halted abruptly, turning to face him with a glare that could cut glass. "Let me make one thing abundantly clear, Mr. Goodrich. I will not tolerate any funny business, any attempts to undermine my contributions, or any further thievery of my work."

Thatcher raised an eyebrow, his expression now more serious. "I assure you, Lady Lottie, I have no intention of taking anything from you. The king's decree forced us into this partnership, nothing more."

She studied him, searching for any sign of insincerity. "Very well, we shall see. But mark my words—if you betray my trust or attempt to pass my work off as your own again, I will expose you for the fraud you truly are."

"Understood. Let it be known that I have no interest in being a fraud. I may have my flaws, but my reputation as a playwright means everything to me."

Their verbal standoff was interrupted by the sounds of actors laughing nearby, their voices carrying through the corridors. Lottie and Thatcher turned and continued their walk, now with a begrudging understanding.

They were, unfortunately, partners.

CHAPTER SIX

MAYFAIR, THE EPITOME of London Society, exuded an air of opulence and elegance. Lottie found herself seated in a lavishly decorated drawing room at Rainville and Nora's townhouse on Upper Brook Street the next day. Her gaze wandered around the room, taking in the intricate details of the wallpaper, the polished wooden furniture, and the vibrant hues of the oil paintings adorning the walls.

She couldn't help but feel a sense of unease, her mind plagued by thoughts of her unexpected collaboration with Thatcher Goodrich. How could she work with a man who had so callously stolen her play? Lottie's usually confident disposition had been shaken.

Rainville reclined in an armchair across from her, his piercing gold eyes studying her intently. Dressed impeccably in a tailored black coat and cravat, he exuded an air of authority that Lottie couldn't help but respect, even though she spent much of her time arguing with him.

"Lady Lottie," he began, "I understand your reservations about working with Mr. Goodrich. However, I must impress upon you the gravity of this opportunity. You would be the first female playwright to write directly for a king, a chance to prove that your talents are superior to Goodrich's."

"But why should I collaborate with a man who has shown such disregard for my work? He's taken credit for *my* play, and now I'm expected to work alongside him?"

Rainville leaned forward, his expression earnest. "Because, my dear, we must remember that the ultimate goal is to create a masterpiece that will impress King William. If we succeed, your name will be forever etched in history, and you will have achieved something truly remarkable. Isn't that what you've wanted?"

Lottie hesitated. The idea of being a trailblazer appealed to her, but the bitterness of Thatcher's betrayal still lingered. "I fear that our styles and creative visions are too dissimilar."

Rainville offered a reassuring smile. "Differences can lead to innovation. You both have unique strengths, and if you can find common ground, your collaboration could result in something truly remarkable."

Nora gracefully entered the room, her emerald-green evening gown accentuating her elegantly curved figure. She joined the conversation. "I must confess, Lottie, I share your worries. This partnership may bring unwanted attention, especially from the Revivalists. Those monsters take offense to extraordinary women."

Lottie furrowed her brow, remembering the recent tales of the Revivalists—noblemen who harbored dangerous and radical beliefs about the natural order of society, often enforced through violence. Her two sisters had barely escaped their clutches. "But Nora, should I let fear dictate my choices as a writer?"

Rainville chimed in, his tone soothing. "We're not asking you to compromise your principles, Lottie. We're merely suggesting that you consider the consequences of your actions. Your work has the power to influence hearts and minds, and that can be a double-edged sword in a society as divided as ours."

Lottie's thoughts were in turmoil. She was torn between her desire to make a mark as a playwright and her concern for the potential dangers lurking in the shadows. Rainville's words held weight, and Nora's apprehension was not unfounded. The Revivalists had left their mark on the Castlebury family.

As she contemplated her decision, she couldn't help but wonder if her idol, London stage actress Dorothea Jordan, had faced similar dilemmas during her time onstage. Lottie was well aware of the courage it took for a woman to step into the limelight, and she couldn't ignore the opportunity that lay before her.

Rainville's gaze remained fixed on her, his conviction unwavering. "Consider the legacy of Dorothea Jordan, Lottie," he said like he had read her mind. "She was not just an actress but a woman who defied societal norms. She captivated the heart of a king and left her mark on history. You have the potential to do the same."

The weight of the decision bore down on her shoulders. She had always admired Dorothea Jordan's courage, but could she muster the same resolve?

Rainville continued, "The world is changing, and women like you, and Carenza, and Nora, are at the forefront of that change. Your words have the power to challenge and inspire. If you decide to work with Mr. Goodrich, you will be taking a step toward a brighter future for all women."

Nora added, "But if you do, there's no telling what the consequences might be. The Revivalists are becoming increasingly bold. I worry for your safety." After what she'd gone through at their horrid hands, Lottie blamed her sister not at all for her fears.

Her heart constricted with the weight of responsibility. She had always felt a burning desire to be recognized for her talents, to break free from the constraints of societal expectations. Now, that opportunity lay before her, but it came with its own set of challenges and dangers.

Rainville stood and approached her, his gold-gazed expression kind but determined. "Think on it, sister. We will support whatever decision you make. But remember that sometimes, the greatest achievements require the bravest choices."

As she watched her sister and brother-in-law, she couldn't help but feel the weight of their expectations and her own ambitions pressing down on her. It was a choice that would shape her destiny and perhaps even the destiny of women who aspired to defy convention. How could she say no?

Lottie's resolve began to strengthen. She recalled the countless hours she had spent alone in her room, pouring her thoughts and creativity into her plays. She couldn't deny that her desire to be recognized as a playwright burned brighter than ever.

Nora's words about the Revivalists did give her pause. She knew the dangerous group and the havoc they wreaked on those who challenged their beliefs. It was a chilling thought to become a potential target. But could she let that small chance stop her? Rainville's mention of Dorothea Jordan resonated with her deeply. The actress had been a beacon of courage in a world that often stifled women's voices. Lottie couldn't help but be inspired by her story, a woman who had blazed a trail for others to follow.

Taking a deep breath, she finally spoke, her voice steady and determined. "You're right, Rainville. This is a chance to make a difference, not just for me but for women like me who dream of a different future. I'll do it."

A warm smile spread across the duke's handsome face, and he reached over and placed a reassuring hand on her shoulder. "That's the spirit, Lottie. I knew you'd make the right choice."

Nora's concern softened into a supportive expression. "You have this under control, sister. Goodrich is temperamental, but a true talent. You can do this."

Lottie nodded. It was a daunting path she had chosen, but it was also a path of potential and change. She would work with Thatcher Goodrich, even if it meant dealing with the infuriating man, and together, they would create a play that would make history. She couldn't deny the thrill of possibility that coursed through her veins at the prospect of challenging societal norms and blazing a trail for women like her.

"Well, now that that's settled, let's head above stairs to assess the state of the new nursery, shall we?"

Lottie's mind kept swirling, but as Nora mentioned the nursery, her thoughts skidded to a halt. *Nursery?* Surely she hadn't heard that correctly. Her sister couldn't possibly be…

"Wait, Nora, are you…expecting?" Lottie's voice was filled with disbelief as she searched her sister's face for confirmation.

Nora chuckled softly, shaking her head. "Heavens no. Not yet, anyway," she replied with a teasing glint in her eye. "But Rainville and I have been discussing the possibility of starting a family soon. We thought it best to prepare in advance. There's been a *lot* of practice."

A rush of warmth flooded Lottie's chest as she realized the implications of Nora's words. Her sister, whom she had watched grow from a carefree, fiery young woman into a devoted wife and soon-to-be mother, was embarking on a new chapter of her life, one filled with the joys and challenges of parenthood. "Oh, I see," she said, a smile playing at her lips. "Well, that's certainly… lovely. I'm sure the nursery will be absolutely charming when it's finished."

Nora beamed, her eyes brimming with excitement. "I'm glad you think so, Lottie. It's all quite thrilling, isn't it? The thought of a little one running about the house."

Lottie nodded, her heart swelling with affection for her sister and her new future. "Indeed, it is," she agreed as they ascended the stairs. "And whenever the time comes, I'll be right here to help you every step of the way."

As they stepped into the nursery, Lottie marveled at the transformation the room would undergo in the coming months. Soft sunlight filtered through the lace curtains, casting a warm glow over the mostly empty space. It was a room filled with the promise of new beginnings, a blank canvas waiting to be painted with the colors of love and laughter. But as she turned to share in the moment with Nora, she noticed a mischievous twinkle in her sister's eye, a hint of excitement dancing beneath the surface. Lottie raised an eyebrow in question, curiosity piqued by her sister's sudden change in demeanor.

Nora let out a soft chuckle, her hand fluttering to her chest in mock innocence. "Oh, let's be honest," she said, her voice dropping to a conspiratorial whisper. "Inspecting the nursery was really just an excuse to escape Rainville's exceptional hearing for a moment, wasn't it?"

Lottie couldn't help but laugh at her sister's candor. "Perhaps," she admitted with a playful grin. "But what's on your mind? You seem positively bursting with excitement."

Nora's eyes danced with trouble as she leaned in closer, her voice barely above a whisper. "You simply must tell me everything about Mr. Goodrich," she exclaimed, her words tumbling out in a rush. "He's so brooding and attractive and mysterious, isn't he? I wonder what secrets lie hidden beneath that enigmatic exterior of his."

Lottie couldn't suppress a chuckle at her sister's eagerness. "Oh, you do have a penchant for drama, don't you?" she teased, shaking her head. "Loath as I am, and as much as I dislike him, I must admit that there is something intriguing about Mr. Goodrich. A certain air of mystery that sets him apart from the others."

Nora's eyes widened with anticipation. "I must know everything,"

And as they settled into two chairs taking up a corner of the nursery, away from prying ears and watchful eyes, Lottie found herself succumbing to her sister's infectious enthusiasm. She leaned in close to Nora, as if afraid that even the walls might betray their secrets. "Well, if you must know, Mr. Goodrich is…vexing," she confessed, her tone laced with frustration. "He's always so inscrutable, with that brooding demeanor of his that's enough to drive anyone to distraction. Also, he's arrogant. Demanding."

"Go on," Nora urged, leaning in closer as if afraid to miss a single detail. "Tell me more."

"His voice is like velvet over sand," Lottie continued. "Smooth and alluring, yet somehow grating at the same time. And don't even get me started on his eyes—they're like the fog that sometimes rolls in on the Thames, all smoky and moody."

As she spoke, Lottie caught herself sighing, her breath catching in her throat at the memory of Thatcher's piercing gaze. She chastised herself for allowing her thoughts to wander in such a direction.

Nora watched her reaction with a knowing smile. "Sounds positively dreadful, Lottie," she teased. "And yet I can't help but sense a hint of...admiration in your words."

Lottie's cheeks flushed with embarrassment at Nora's astute observation. "Nonsense," she protested, though her heart hammered in her chest at the thought of Thatcher's enigmatic allure. Her words tumbled out in a rush, her frustration palpable in every syllable. Because as handsome as he may be, it still rang true. "He's awful, Nora. A liar with no morals, like a hedonistic man of the world," she declared vehemently. Perhaps *too* vehemently? "And I can assure you, that holds no appeal to me whatsoever. No matter how mysterious or handsome he may be."

Nora regarded her with a knowing look. It was clear that she could see the conflict raging within Lottie. "I understand your reservations," she began gently. "But sometimes, the most intriguing individuals are those who defy our expectations, who challenge us to see beyond the surface to the depths beneath."

"You don't understand," Lottie insisted. "He's not someone I could ever—"

But before she could finish her sentence, Nora reached out and placed a comforting hand on her arm. "Darling, I'm not asking you to fall in love with Mr. Goodrich," she said softly. "But perhaps there's more to him than meets the eye. Perhaps, in working together, you'll discover a side of him you never knew existed."

Lottie knew Nora meant well, but the thought of delving deeper into Thatcher Goodrich's mysterious world filled her with a sense of unease. "Perhaps," she conceded reluctantly. "But I make no promises, Nora. My opinion of him remains unchanged."

Nora nodded. "Of course. You needn't do anything you're not comfortable with," she reassured her sister. "Just remember, sometimes the greatest discoveries are made when we least expect them."

They turned their attention back to the nursery, the room filled with the soft glow of sunlight and the promise of new beginnings, and Lottie wondered what secrets lay hidden within the heart of Thatcher, and whether she was truly prepared to uncover them.

"For instance," her sister started casually, "there's the discovery of how incredibly tempting he is."

Lottie's cheeks flushed. "Nora, please," she scoffed, though there was a hint of sheepishness in her voice. "His...attractiveness has nothing to do with it."

"Come now. You can't deny that his good looks and charm do make the burden of working with him a little less difficult to bear, can you?"

Lottie's jaw tightened as she struggled to find a suitable retort. But deep down, she knew that Nora was right. As much as she hated to admit it, there was a certain *something* to Thatcher that she couldn't quite shake. "I-I suppose. But that doesn't change the fact that he's...he's ..." Her words faltered as her thoughts drifted once more to Thatcher's dark good looks and the enigmatic aura that surrounded him like a shroud. She couldn't deny the way her heart raced at the mere thought of him.

And as she caught herself sighing again, her consternation only deepened. How could she allow herself to be so affected by a man she despised?

Nora watched her internal struggle. "Oh, Lottie," she murmured. "Love is a strange and unpredictable thing, isn't it?"

Lottie snapped her spine straight. "Who said anything about love?" she blurted. "I've been talking about writing."

"Of course—my mistake," Nora replied breezily, a small smile still upon her lips.

"Indeed," Lottie replied, suddenly prickly and hot inside.

Pushing from the chair, she made for the doorway. "Now, I must be on my way."

"I'll see you out." Her sister rose from her chair and followed.

As Lottie left Rainville and Nora's townhouse, she couldn't help but feel conflicted. She had taken the first step toward a future that held both promise and danger, working with Goodrich on this play while the Revivalists were still loose, but she was determined to see it through.

CHAPTER SEVEN

THATCHER SAT AT his cluttered desk, eyes locked on the blank parchment before him. The room felt stifling, suffocating, as if the walls themselves were closing in on him. He dipped his quill into the inkwell and then hesitated, the tip hovering above the paper. Lady Lottie's presence in the office had done little to alleviate his inner turmoil. If anything, her mere existence seemed to amplify the maelstrom of frustration that churned within him. She was, after all, the reason he found himself in this predicament, tasked with co-writing a play when his creativity had abandoned him.

Across the desk, Lottie sat with an expectant look, her wheat-colored hair cascading around her shoulders like a golden waterfall. The silence between them had stretched into an uncomfortable abyss, broken only by the scratching of his quill as he idly doodled on the parchment.

Lottie cleared her throat. "Mr. Goodrich, perhaps we should start with the plot. What direction do you envision for our play?"

Thatcher's jaw tightened, his frustration boiling beneath the surface. He knew he should have had a plan, a concept, something to guide them. But the creative wellspring within him had run dry, leaving nothing but a desolate wasteland of ideas. "Let's…" he began, his voice tight with irritation. "Let's start with the characters. Who are they? What are their motivations?"

Anything. Come on, give me something at all to work with, to spark my creativity once more. Please.

Lottie regarded him with a mixture of patience and exasperation. "I suppose that's a good place to begin. I was thinking of a strong-willed heroine who defies societal expectations, much like myself."

Thatcher forced himself to nod, though her words felt like a weight upon his chest. He had always been adept at crafting compelling characters, but today, his mind remained obstinately blank. He dipped his quill into the inkwell again and made a futile attempt to sketch an outline. Minutes ticked by in agonizing silence as they attempted to brainstorm ideas, but each suggestion felt forced and uninspired. Thatcher's frustration grew with every passing second, but he couldn't bring himself to admit his creative block to Lottie. To do so would be to acknowledge his vulnerability, something he had carefully concealed for years.

Lottie leaned forward, her gaze fixed on the parchment, her expression thoughtful. "What if our heroine is a playwright, much like myself? She faces obstacles and prejudices in a male-dominated world but refuses to yield to convention."

Thatcher's irritation flared, and he snapped, "And what if we're merely writing your life story, Lady Lottie?"

The words hung in the air, charged with tension. Lottie's eyes blazed with indignation. "Mr. Goodrich, I have had enough of your obstinacy and arrogance. If you cannot put aside your petty grievances, then perhaps we should abandon this collaboration altogether."

Thatcher felt a pang of regret as he watched her rise from her chair, her determination evident in every graceful movement. He knew he had pushed her too far, but he couldn't bring himself to apologize, not when his own frustration threatened to consume him. With a curt nod, Lottie turned and walked toward the door. Before she could reach it, however, Thatcher called out, his voice tinged with resignation, "Wait."

She paused but didn't turn around, her back ramrod straight. "What is it, Mr. Goodrich?"

He sighed, his shoulders sagging with defeat. "I'm sorry. My temper got the best of me. I... I am struggling with this collaboration more than I care to admit."

Lottie slowly turned to face him, her gaze softening. "We're in this together, Mr. Goodrich, whether we like it or not. But if we're to create something worthwhile, we must find a way to work together."

Thatcher nodded, a begrudging acknowledgment of the truth in her words. "Agreed. Let's start fresh, shall we? And please, call me Thatcher." He could no longer bear the stifling atmosphere of the theatre. His head throbbed with frustration, and the constant presence of Lady Lottie felt like a lead weight around his neck. He needed air—fresh, unencumbered air to clear his thoughts and, just maybe, rekindle the spark of inspiration that had eluded him.

Pushing his chair back with a harsh scrape against the floor, he stood abruptly. "I need some air," he declared. Without waiting for Lottie's response, he strode toward the door, leaving her momentarily stunned in his wake. She watched him with a mixture of disbelief and irritation. Surely she had expected their collaboration to be challenging. But he was certain she had not anticipated his sheer willfulness.

With a sigh, Lottie rose from her seat and followed after him. They emerged from the theatre into a glorious autumn day. The sky stretched overhead, an unbroken expanse of azure, while the trees wore their autumnal attire of burnished gold and fiery red. The air carried a crispness that invigorated the senses.

Thatcher hailed a waiting hack, and the driver tipped his hat respectfully as they climbed aboard. Once inside, he leaned back against the plush seats, his frustration seemingly forgotten for the moment. "Hyde Park," he instructed the driver tersely.

As he settled into the bench seat of the hack beside Lottie, a sense of calm washed over him, smoothing his agitation. The bustling energy of Covent Garden gradually faded into the background as they made their way through the heart of London.

The hack rattled along the cobblestone streets, the rhythmic clatter blending with the noise of the city. Thatcher's gaze wandered, taking in the sights and sounds. Buildings of various architectural styles lined the streets, their façades a testament to the city's rich history and cultural diversity. From elegant townhouses adorned with intricate wrought-iron balconies to bustling market stalls teeming with colorful produce, every corner held a story waiting to be discovered.

But it was the people who truly brought the city to life. Merchants haggled with customers over prices, children played in the streets with unabashed joy, and fashionable ladies and gentlemen strolled arm in arm, their laughter mingling with the crisp autumn air.

Beside him, Lottie sat bathed in sunlight, her features illuminated by the soft golden glow. Her hair shone like spun silk, catching the light in a cascade of shimmering waves. Thatcher admired the way the sunlight danced across her rose-and-cream complexion. Damn, but her skin had a radiant glow.

Her presence was magnetic, drawing his gaze like a moth to a flame. Despite her outward strength, there was a softness to her, a vulnerability hidden beneath the surface. Thatcher found himself captivated by the juxtaposition of her solid, statuesque frame and the delicate grace with which she carried herself.

As they passed through the affluent neighborhoods near the park, Thatcher's senses were overwhelmed by the opulence and wealth that surrounded them. Imposing townhouses with grandiose façades stood tall against the backdrop of the clear blue sky, their windows gleaming. The grandeur of their surroundings served as a stark reminder of the life he might have had, had fate dealt him a different hand.

As a baron's son, he should have been no stranger to such luxury and privilege. The thought brought a grumble to his lips and a scowl to his brow as he contemplated the paths not taken and the dreams left unfulfilled.

Third son of an impoverished baron.

Lavish would not describe his upbringing.

Thatcher's gaze inevitably drifted back to Lottie, her presence beside him a vivid reminder of the unexpected turns life could take. He felt a twinge of regret at the thought of what might have been had his father not been what he was, but he quickly shook it off, refusing to dwell on the past.

Instead, he focused on the present, and the jarring fact that even with the splendor of their current surroundings, it was Lottie who captured his attention.

⤞⤞⤞⤛⤛⤛

LOTTIE COULDN'T HELP but marvel at the beauty of the day. She had always found solace in the natural world, and this unexpected detour offered her a brief respite from the stifling confines of the theatre. "It's a lovely day," she remarked.

Thatcher glanced at her briefly, his brooding demeanor momentarily softened by the serene surroundings. "Yes," he admitted, though it was clear that he was not yet willing to relinquish his gruff exterior. "The park has always been a place of solace for me."

As the hack rattled along the cobbled streets toward Hyde Park, Lottie couldn't help but steal glances at him. There was something about him, something she couldn't quite put her finger on. Beneath the layers of arrogance and frustration, she sensed a depth of vulnerability that piqued her curiosity. One she hadn't noticed before.

When they arrived at their destination, they stepped out of the carriage onto the sun-dappled path. The park was abuzz with activity—couples strolled hand in hand, children played near the pond, and the distant sound of music drifted from a nearby bandstand. It was a picture of idyllic London life.

She saw Thatcher take a deep breath, inhaling the crisp autumn air as if it were a lifeline. His features, which had been etched with tension, relaxed ever so slightly. "This is what I needed," he admitted, surprising Lottie with his candor.

She smiled, her earlier annoyance giving way to a sense of camaraderie. "Sometimes, a change of scenery can do wonders for the soul."

They walked along the path, the swish of their footsteps mingling with the rustling leaves underfoot. It was a comfortable silence, unburdened by the weight of words. Lottie stole sidelong glances at Thatcher, taking in the sharp lines of his profile and the way the sunlight played on his dark hair. The playwright seemed lost in thought. The bustling world of the park seemed to fade away, leaving just the two of them in a tranquil bubble of existence. It was a peculiar sensation, one that left her feeling strangely vulnerable yet undeniably alive.

As they strolled, the day unfurled before them, an unexpected respite from the pressures of their collaboration. It was a moment of peace, of shared silence, and perhaps, just perhaps, the beginning of an understanding between two fiercely independent souls, Lottie thought. Hoped.

She followed him as they ventured deeper into Hyde Park, away from the bustling crowds. They walked along the path that skirted the Serpentine, and the tranquil waters of the lake shimmered in the autumn sunlight. A gentle breeze ruffled the surface, creating mesmerizing patterns on the water.

Thatcher's steps slowed as he gazed out at the serene expanse of the lake. "This place," he said, his voice low and contemplative, "this is where I often come when I need to think, to find inspiration."

Lottie joined him by the water's edge. "It's breathtaking," she admitted. She couldn't deny the allure of the spot he had chosen. "Do you find it helps you write?"

Thatcher nodded. "There's something about the tranquility of this place that clears my mind. It's as if the stillness here allows my thoughts to flow more freely."

As they stood side by side, the weight of their argument from earlier seemed to dissipate. The presence of nature had a way of mending fractured spirits. Thatcher reached into his coat pocket and pulled out a leather-bound notebook and a quill. "This is where we'll work," he declared, choosing a nearby bench overlooking the water. He settled down, the notebook open on his lap, and motioned for Lottie to join him. "A change of scenery might be just what we need to tap our creative wells."

Lottie hesitated for a moment, then took a seat beside him. She watched as he dipped the quill into an inkwell and brought it to the page. "So, where do we begin?" she asked, her curiosity piqued. It was interesting, learning another writer's techniques.

Thatcher's brow furrowed as he stared at the blank page. "That's the problem, isn't it? We have the opportunity of a lifetime to write a play for the king himself, and yet…we've got nothing."

Lottie regarded him thoughtfully. She had seen his talent firsthand, witnessed the power of his words on the stage. She hated to admit it, but… "You're an exceptional playwright, Thatcher. This is merely a slow start. We should begin with something simple, a scene, a character. Let the rest flow from there."

His smoky eyes met hers. There was a vulnerability in his gaze, a crack in the armor he wore so well. "You make it sound so easy."

"It doesn't have to be easy," she replied with a small smile. "We'll figure it out together."

And that was how she found herself in a secluded corner by the Serpentine, with the tranquil waters glistening under the late afternoon sun. They had settled on a moss-covered bench, and she couldn't help but appreciate the beauty of their surroundings. It was as if nature itself had conspired to inspire them.

"Much better," Thatcher declared. He cast a sidelong glance at Lottie. "I believe we've found the ideal place to work."

Lottie smiled. "I must admit that this location has a certain charm. Now, shall we begin?" With pen poised, she turned her attention to him. "Let's start with the opening scene," she suggested. "What do you envision?" Her gaze shifted fixed on the lake as her thoughts drifted. "I see a moonlit garden, shrouded in mystery. A solitary figure, cloaked in shadows, stands beneath an ancient oak tree. She's waiting for someone, but she doesn't know if they'll ever come."

He listened intently, looking captivated by her words. "Intriguing," he mused. "Who is this figure waiting for, and why?"

Lottie's pen moved across the page as she began to sketch the scene. "She's a woman of strength and independence, but she carries a secret deep within her. The person she's waiting for holds the key to her heart, yet they're both entangled in a web of intrigue and danger."

"A forbidden love," Thatcher ventured, "set against a backdrop of political turmoil and betrayal. The stakes couldn't be higher."

"Exactly. And as they navigate treacherous waters, they'll discover that love has the power to overcome even the darkest of secrets."

CHAPTER EIGHT

THE SUN BATHED Hyde Park in a warm, golden glow, casting dappled shadows beneath the rustling leaves of the ancient trees. Lottie and Thatcher had moved from the bench and sat side by side on a blanket, their scripts spread out before them. The soft breeze carried the sweet scent of autumn leaves and the distant laughter of children playing. Yet despite the idyllic surroundings, an undercurrent of tension hung in the air.

Lottie scrutinized Thatcher as he sketched a lazy pattern in the grass with his finger, avoiding her gaze. She couldn't shake the feeling that something was amiss, that there was more to his reluctance to collaborate than met the eye. "Why are you avoiding my questions, Thatcher?" she said, finally breaking the silence.

He glanced at her briefly, his moody, enigmatic eyes filled with an inscrutable mixture of emotions. "I'm not avoiding anything, my lady," he replied, his voice smooth and composed. "I'm merely considering the best approach to our play."

Lottie's skepticism deepened. She had expected their collaboration to be challenging, but she hadn't anticipated Thatcher's evasiveness. "Considering, or stalling?" she countered.

Thatcher leaned back on one elbow, his lips curling into a sly smile. "Perhaps a bit of both," he admitted.

Lottie's cheeks flushed with a mix of irritation and determination. She refused to let Thatcher undermine her confidence. "I didn't agree to work on this play to watch you twirl your quill and make idle conversation," she declared. "I want to create something remarkable, something that will captivate the audience, and mesmerize the king. But I can't do that if you keep evading my questions."

Thatcher's smile faded, and he regarded her with a newfound intensity. "Remarkable, you say?" he said, taking on a more serious tone. "Very well, let's discuss our play. What are your thoughts on the central conflict of our story?"

Lottie seized the opportunity to redirect their conversation toward their shared project. She leaned forward. "I envision a clash of ideologies," she began, her words flowing with enthusiasm. "A struggle between tradition and progress, where our characters are torn between the constraints of Society and their desire for personal freedom."

She observed Thatcher closely. He seemed to be dancing around the plot, avoiding her questions and scoffing at her ideas. She couldn't ignore the nagging feeling that something was amiss, that Thatcher was hiding something from her. He continued to avoid concrete suggestions.

Lottie's patience wore even thinner, and she couldn't help but feel that he was hiding something from her. "Thatcher," she said, her frustration clear, "why won't you just work with me? This is something we both must do."

⟫⟫⟩⟨⟨⟨

THATCHER, INSTEAD OF confessing his writer's block, chose to feed her a string of lies, trying to charm and distract her. He leaned in closer. "Lady Lottie, there's something you should know," he whispered. "I find myself rather distracted in your presence. Your beauty, your wit—it's all quite overwhelming."

Lottie raised an eyebrow, not falling for his ploy. "Mr. Goodrich, this is hardly the time for such distractions," she replied. "We have work to do."

Thatcher's smile only widened as he leaned in closer, danger-ously close to her lips. "It's Thatcher," he murmured. "Sometimes a touch of distraction can lead to unexpected inspiration."

She leaned in closer, her lips tantalizingly close to his, and batted her eyelashes with exaggerated coyness. "Why, Thatcher, are you suggesting that we should indulge in distractions for the sake of inspiration?" she replied in a sultry tone, her fingers lightly tracing patterns on his arm.

Thatcher's eyes widened slightly. He had not expected her to reciprocate his flirtation. He had thought to disconcert her, but instead, the tables seemed to have turned. His voice grew huskier as he played along. "I must confess, I find your proposal rather tempting," he murmured, moving his hand closer to hers.

A small chuckle escaped her lips. Christ, he enjoyed this play-ful banter.

"Oh, Thatcher, we wouldn't want our collaboration to suffer because of distractions, would we?" she teased.

He chuckled, the tension between them momentarily forgot-ten. "Very well, let's save the distractions for later," he conceded, leaning back and returning to a more serious demeanor.

Lottie was obviously satisfied that she had managed to redi-rect their focus to the task at hand. He could tell that she knew there was something amiss with him, but for now, she would let him believe that she had fallen for his charming distractions.

Foolish him, he'd take it.

➤≫≪≪

BACK AND FORTH it went, Thatcher unable to engage his mind in any substantive way to produce words worth a shilling. He blamed it on the sunlight and the woman sitting next to him. "Stop trying to make this play about you. This is the tenth version of a female attempting to corrupt the male-dominated structures of society that you've mentioned. Matters of the heart, I tell you—that is what the people want."

"And I suppose you know about matters of the heart?"

"Enough to write about it, certainly."

"Really?" she asked, tipping her head to the side as she gazed at him thoughtfully. "Have you ever been in love?"

The question jolted him right in the chest. "I, um," he started, but struggled to find his voice.

She looked away. "That's what I thought."

Was that dismissal? Had she just *dismissed* him?

This lady knew nothing. "Her name was Fiona," he answered quietly. Honestly. Why, he wasn't sure. "I was not yet twenty, but I offered her father everything I had in exchange for her hand."

"What happened?"

"Nothing." Thatcher shrugged. "My everything wasn't enough. Her father married her to the second son of a baronet soon after, and I never saw her again."

Silence hung in the autumn air for several heartbeats.

"I'm sorry that happened to you. That sounds awful."

Thatcher shrugged again. "It was a long time ago. I'm well past it."

"Still…" The look she gave him had his breath catching in his chest.

"It's all right," he murmured, unable to take his gaze from hers.

In a blink she closed the distance, and her lips met his, lush and full of innocence.

"Lottie," he growled, and drove his fingers into her thick, glossy hair to hold her steady. Taking the lead, he lightly swept his tongue against the seam of her lips, inviting her to open for him.

Open for him, she did. With her hands gripping his wrists, Thatcher felt her melt into him, her body ripe and firm and perfect against his. Her head tipped further back as she clung to him and made sweet sighing sounds. Sounds he would replay over and over in his mind later in the privacy of his bedchamber.

He explored her mouth, memorized her taste. Rich and robust and darkly sweet. Oh, so very sweet. "Lottie," he whispered roughly against her kiss-swollen lips. "I want to touch you everywhere."

She released a long, dreamy sigh and leaned in for another kiss. "That sounds nice." Her lips, so warm and plush, met his once more.

Everything inside him seized as lust sprang from deep within and poured through his body like molten metal. "Careful," he warned. She had no idea how much he desired to do just that. Right there in Hyde Park.

Thatcher wanted nothing more than to stretch her naked body out in the grass and touch her, *taste* her, everywhere.

Everywhere.

"Runaway dogs!" a shrill voice cried, shocking him from his primal inclinations and needs.

"What?" Lottie mumbled, her voice slurred with the headiness of passion.

"What the devil?" Thatcher glanced over her shoulder and gasped. "Get down!" he demanded, wrapping his arm around her shoulder and dragging her to the grass. "Shite," he cursed. "Shite!"

At least twenty dogs were headed their way at a dead run.

Covering her with his body, Thatcher did his best to protect her from the rogue dog pack. "Don't move," he said into the crook of her neck. With luck they would run right around them and he and Lottie wouldn't be trampled.

"Runaway dogs! Beware!" cried the voice again, closer this time. "They're after that rabbit!"

A fuzzy blur shot by the corner of Thatcher's vision, and he braced for the thunder of paws soon to follow. They came within moments, the dogs determined to chase down their prey. "It's okay," he assured Lottie as he felt her tremble beneath him. "I won't let them hurt you."

Barking and thundering paws surrounded them as the dog pack descended upon them.

"King's dogs, everyone! Runaway dogs!" The voice came from right next to them now as someone huffed and panted their way past. "Oh, I'm in so much trouble for this! Chester, why can't you stop? You're the lead dog!"

Thatcher's shoulders began to shake as laughter bubbled up in his chest, replacing the sense of alarm.

"Bad dog! You're a bad dog, Chester!" the voice called out as the pack raced off through Hyde Park.

Lottie chuckled beneath him. "Well, that was exciting,"

"It most certainly..." Thatcher trailed off when he realized one of his hands was covering her breast. Her very shapely and full breast. "...was," he finished lamely. Quite suddenly his mouth felt dry.

"You can get off me now."

He could. He should. Yes, he most definitely should.

But he didn't *want* to.

CHAPTER NINE

THATCHER SAT ALONE in the sparsely lit room of his town-home, a small and shabby dwelling tucked away in a corner of London that had seen better days. Faded tapestries clung threadbare to the walls, bearing witness to a time when the Goodrich family had known wealth and status. Now, only a few pieces of well-worn furniture remained, surrounded by the echoes of faded memories.

His cook and valet—well, his man-of-all-work, truthfully—a tough and brooding older man who had fought against Napoleon on the Continent, moved quietly about the room. The clinking of dishes and the crackling of the fireplace provided a comforting backdrop to Thatcher's solitary musings.

Thatcher himself was a man of contrasts. At thirty, he bore the weight of experience in his smoky eyes and the lines etched on his face. His raven-black hair framed a countenance that often wore an enigmatic mask. He was not a man who readily shared his past or his emotions, preferring to bury them beneath layers of wit and cynicism. The son of a lowly drunkard peer, Thatcher had grown up with the harsh reality of limited resources and shattered dreams. He was the youngest of his siblings, born into a family that had long since squandered their noble inheritance. His father's vices had left them destitute, and young Thatcher had quickly learned that survival meant using his wits and words as weapons and defense. He had scraped by, living like a poor artist, penniless and hungry. His sharp tongue and keen insight had become his only assets, allowing him to earn a meager living through his writing. Those early years had been marked by hardship and uncertainty, but they had also forged him into a man who could navigate the treacherous waters of London's High Society with ease.

His rise to prominence as a playwright had been a long and arduous journey, filled with rejection, disappointment, and relentless determination. He had clawed his way up from the bottom, overcoming the skepticism of the elite theatre world that had seen him as an upstart with no pedigree.

Now, seated at his worn wooden desk, a flickering lamp casting a warm glow over the parchment before him, Thatcher wrote furiously. His quill scratched across the paper, leaving behind a trail of ink that would soon become his latest contribution to his and Lottie's play. For once, the words flowed from his mind to the page, a torrent of ideas and emotions that had been building up inside him.

Writing was his refuge, his sanctuary from the harsh realities of his past and the weight of his ambitions. It was his way of dealing with the hardships he had endured, a way to channel his frustrations and insecurities into something beautiful and profound. Through his words, he could create worlds and characters that transcended the limitations of his own life.

As he wrote, Thatcher lost himself in the world of their play, and the characters came to life in his mind. He became so engrossed in his work that he momentarily forgot the small, shabby room around him and the lonely hours of the evening.

The soft voice of his man, Simms, broke through the silence of the room. "Another late evening of work, eh?" Simms's tone held a mixture of concern and familiarity as he approached the desk with a tray bearing a meal.

Thatcher paused in his writing, setting down his quill and taking a deep breath. "Yes," he replied, his voice tinged with weariness. "The creative muse strikes at the most inconvenient of hours, it seems. But at least she's bloody striking again."

Simms placed the tray on the desk, revealing a hearty plate of roasted chicken and a steaming bowl of vegetable soup. "You ought to take better care of yourself," he admonished gently, his weathered face creased with worry lines. "You can't keep burning the midnight oil like this."

Thatcher chuckled wryly, a faint smile touching his lips. "Ah, you sound like my mother. She used to say the same thing when I was a boy."

The older man's eyes softened with understanding. "Your mother was a wise woman, sir," he replied. "She knew the importance of balance in a man's life."

Thatcher's smile faded as he picked up his fork and began to eat. The food was simple but comforting, and he appreciated Simms's efforts to look after him. "Balance is a luxury I can ill afford, my friend," he admitted quietly. "Not when I've come this far."

Simms leaned against the desk. "You've worked hard to get where you are. I've seen it myself," he said. "But don't forget to live a little along the way. There's more to life than the stage and the applause of the crowd and making coin to pay off your father's debts."

Thatcher's eyes met Simms's, and for a moment, he felt a pang of longing for the simple pleasures he had sacrificed in his pursuit of success. "Perhaps you're right," he conceded, his voice softer than usual.

As he continued to eat, Thatcher's mind drifted back to Lady Lottie and the unusual partnership that had been thrust upon him. He couldn't deny the intrigue she stirred within him, both as a woman and as a writer. There was a fire in her eyes, a determination to prove herself in a world that often dismissed the talents of women. He experienced far more attraction to the woman than he well should.

"Thatcher." Simms's voice interrupted his thoughts, bringing him back to the present. "Is there something troubling you?"

Thatcher hesitated, unsure of how much to reveal to his loyal servant. "It's nothing, Simms," he replied evasively. "Just the usual challenges of creative endeavors."

Simms studied him for a moment, as if sensing there was more beneath the surface. "If you ever need to talk, sir, I'm here," he said quietly before retreating to the shadows of the room, leaving Thatcher to his thoughts.

Alone once more, Thatcher returned to his writing, the words flowing more smoothly now. But as he crafted the dialogue between his characters, he couldn't help but wonder how this unexpected collaboration with Lady Lottie would change the course of his life and whether it would ultimately lead to the recognition and fulfillment he had long sought. His quill scratched across the paper, but his thoughts were far from the words he penned. Her image lingered in his mind, her striking blue eyes and fiery spirit refusing to be ignored. He couldn't deny the attraction that simmered between them, like a slow-burning fuse threatening to ignite.

The notion of a romantic entanglement was both tempting and treacherous. He had always prided himself on his self-control, on not allowing emotions to cloud his judgment. But there was something about Lottie that unsettled him, that made him question the carefully constructed walls he had built around his heart.

With a frustrated sigh, he set his quill aside and ran a hand through his disheveled hair. This was absurd, he scolded himself. He had no time for distractions, especially not the romantic kind. His focus should be on the play, on making it a success that would secure his place in the world of theatre. But try as he might to push those thoughts away, they persisted. He couldn't help wondering what it would be like to hold Lottie in his arms, to taste the sweetness of her lips. It was a dangerous fantasy, one that threatened to consume him if he allowed it to take root.

With a sharp shake of his head, Thatcher forced himself to return to his writing. He berated himself for such frivolous daydreams, for allowing a woman to distract him from his work. It was a weakness he couldn't afford, not in his line of business.

As the night wore on, the lamp burned lower, casting long shadows in the dimly lit room. Thatcher's determination to finish his work grew stronger, fueled by his irritation at his own wayward thoughts. He couldn't let himself be swayed by romantic notions, not when there was so much at stake. But deep down, he couldn't deny the spark that had ignited between him and Lady Lottie. It was a fire he would need to keep carefully controlled, lest it consume them both. And so he resolved to focus on the play, to channel his passion into his work, and to keep the dangerous allure of romance at bay.

With renewed fervor, he was determined to create a master-piece that would overshadow all distractions, no matter how tempting they might be. The room was stifling, and the pressure to produce weighed heavily on Thatcher's shoulders. He dipped his quill into the inkwell and brought it to the parchment, but as hard as he tried, no words flowed. They had dried up once again. The blank page mocked him, a stark reminder of his own inadequacy.

Frustration welled up inside him, and he slammed the quill down onto the desk. The ink splattered, forming an ugly blot on the paper. "Damn it," he muttered to himself, running his hands through his hair in agitation. It was as if the harder he tried, the more elusive inspiration became. His mind again felt like a barren wasteland, devoid of any creative spark.

"Is everything all right, sir?" Simms inquired from down the hall.

Thatcher sighed heavily, his frustration giving way to a sense of defeat. "No, blast it," he admitted. "It's as if my mind has gone completely blank once again."

Simms, ever the practical and loyal servant, entered the room and offered a suggestion. "Perhaps a walk might clear your head, sir? Some fresh air might do you good."

Thatcher considered the idea for a moment. He knew he

needed to step away from his desk, to break free from the suffocating grip of his own thoughts. With a nod, he agreed, "You may be right. A walk could be just what I need." He rose from his chair and donned his coat, preparing to venture out into the cool night air. Perhaps a change of scenery would help him break through this new creative block, and he could return to his work with a fresh perspective.

As he made his way to the door, he felt a twinge of frustration and disappointment. He had always prided himself on his ability to craft stories, to bring characters to life with his words. But it seemed that talent had deserted him yet again, leaving him adrift in a sea of uncertainty and self-doubt. Bloody fun, that.

With a heavy heart, he stepped out into the night, determined to find the inspiration he so desperately needed.

→》》≪《←

LATER, THATCHER STEPPED into Flatt's Gym, a dimly lit space in the heart of Covent Garden. The familiar sounds of grunting, the thuds of punches landing, and the cheers of the spectators welcomed him. He had come here seeking a brief escape from his renewed writer's block, and the gym had never failed to provide both distraction and inspiration.

Sometimes all a man needed was a fist upside the head. Rattled things about and cleared the thoughts.

In the center of the ring, two bare-knuckle boxers sparred with a controlled violence that was both captivating and brutal. The crowd gathered around the ring roared with enthusiasm, their voices blending into a symphony of support and excitement.

His eyes were drawn to one of the boxers, a giant of a man with fiery auburn hair that seemed to catch fire under the dim lighting. Thatcher recognized him instantly, for he was a friend through Rainville, who had brought them together. The boxer moved with a graceful ferocity, his punches a testament to his skill and power. Each strike landed with precision and force, and Thatcher couldn't help but be captivated by the sheer athleticism and determination on display.

As the bout unfolded, it became increasingly clear that the opponent was outmatched. The inevitable outcome drew nearer with each passing second, and the crowd's cheers grew even louder, urging the auburn-haired fighter on. With a final, thunderous punch, the giant delivered the knockout blow, sending his opponent sprawling to the canvas. The gym erupted in cheers and applause, and the victorious boxer raised his arms in triumph, a grin of satisfaction on his bloodied face.

Thatcher joined in the applause, genuinely impressed by the performance he had just witnessed. As the gym began to clear out, he approached the victorious fighter, a sense of camaraderie between them due to their connection through Rainville.

"Bravo, Aaron," Thatcher called out, his voice carrying over the bustling gym. "That was an impressive victory."

The boxer turned to him, his hazel eyes filled with a mix of pride and exhaustion. "Thatcher Goodrich," he said, offering a crooked grin. "Never thought I'd see you here again after I bested your arse into utter humiliation last time."

Thatcher chuckled, shaking his head. "Well, my rather pathetic performance aside, your place is a welcome escape from my own battles," he replied. "You were magnificent in there."

Aaron Longfellow wiped sweat and blood from his face with a cloth as they exchanged pleasantries then chatted about the evening's match and shared stories of their daily lives. Thatcher appreciated the value of such straightforward friendships. In the worlds of theatre and bare-knuckle boxing, they had discovered an unlikely but steadfast kinship.

Aaron's grin widened as he wiped more blood from his face, revealing a set of teeth that seemed to gleam even in the low light of the gym. "You know, playwright," he said, his tone playful, "I've seen you wield words like a master swordsman. How about trying your hand at something a bit more physical? How about another round?"

Thatcher chuckled, the offer both tempting and daunting. He had never been much of a boxer, his talents lying in the realm of words and wit rather than fists and brawn. "As much as I'd love to," he drawled, "We know that I'm no match for you in the ring. I'll stick to my quill and ink for now."

Aaron laughed heartily, slapping Thatcher on the back with a firm hand that seemed twice the size of his own. "Fair enough," he conceded. "But the offer stands if you ever change your mind. It's always good to have a backup plan, especially in the rough-and-tumble world of the theatre."

Thatcher nodded appreciatively. "Indeed," he agreed. "And if you ever find yourself in need of a cleverly crafted line or two, you know where to find me."

With a final exchange of friendly banter, Thatcher bade farewell to Aaron and the gym, leaving behind the exhilarating world of boxing for the quieter, more contemplative realm of words and stories. As he left Flatt's Gym, the lively sounds of the boxing match still echoing in his ears, inspiration rose in him, bolstered by the display of raw determination and skill he had witnessed that evening.

Night blanketed London. The gas lamps lining the cobbled streets flickered in the dark, casting an amber glow that painted the buildings and cobblestones in a soft, ethereal light. He walked on, taking in the intoxicating blend of scents that wafted from the food vendors and flower stalls. The air was thick with the aroma of freshly baked bread, roasting chestnuts, and exotic spices. It was a sensory tapestry that spoke of life and vibrancy, a stark contrast to the quiet solitude of his thoughts.

Thatcher passed by bustling theatres, their marquees aglow with the promise of captivating performances. Actors and actresses in elaborate costumes hurried to their respective venues, their laughter and animated conversations filling the night air. The city seemed to come alive after dark, its pulse quickening with a vibrant energy.

As he strolled, Thatcher couldn't help but feel like a character in one of his own plays, moving through a world of endless possibilities and hidden secrets. London, with its dark alleys and grand boulevards, had always been a source of inspiration for him, a place where stories lurked around every corner.

Finally, he arrived back at his modest townhouse, nestled in a quiet corner of a once sought-after neighborhood. The faded grandeur of the building was evident in the chipped paint and weathered stone, a testament to its neglected history. Inside, the atmosphere was cozy and inviting, with antique furnishings and well-worn books lining the shelves.

Thatcher settled back into his study, a room filled with the scent of aged leather and old parchment. He sat down, his quill poised over a blank sheet of parchment, ready to pour his thoughts onto the page. But as he dipped the quill into the inkwell, images of Lottie filled his mind once more. The memory of her quiet determination, her piercing blue eyes, and the spirited way she spoke about their collaboration lingered in his thoughts. He couldn't escape the feeling that she was a force to be reckoned with, a woman who refused to be ignored.

Unable to resist the urge, Thatcher began to write, letting his imagination carry him away into a world of moonlit meadows and mischievous fairies. The words flowed effortlessly, and he lost himself in the act of creation. It was a refuge, a place where he could escape the demands of the world and find solace in the magic of storytelling.

The hours slipped away, and the first light of dawn began to seep through the curtains. Thatcher blinked, realizing that he had written through the night. He looked down at the pages covered in his words, a sense of accomplishment and fulfillment washing over him. It was in these moments, amidst the quiet solitude of his study, that he truly felt alive.

His gaze lingered on the words, and a sinking feeling settled in the pit of his stomach. The character he had crafted so vividly, a fair maiden in a moonlit meadow, bore an uncanny resemblance to Lottie. He had described her without even realizing it, and now he couldn't un-see the image.

Frustration and anger welled up inside him. How could he have been so foolish, so careless, as to let his thoughts wander in that direction? He berated himself for allowing his mind to conjure such intimate imagery, for blurring the line between reality and fiction. With a frustrated sigh, he pushed his chair back from the desk and ran a hand through his disheveled hair. The ink on his fingers smudged as he scrubbed his face, as if trying to wipe away the unwanted thoughts. It was maddening, this inexplicable attraction he felt toward Lottie.

Thatcher had always prided himself in his discipline and control, both in his writing and in his personal life. But Lottie seemed to unravel him with every encounter, and he despised the way she made him feel—vulnerable, exposed, and utterly out of control. He couldn't deny that there was a magnetic pull between them, a simmering tension that had been building since their first heated exchange. But he had no room for distractions, especially one as beguiling as Lady Lottie.

As the realization of his folly settled in, Thatcher clenched his jaw in frustration. He knew he needed to focus on their collaboration, to deliver a play that would satisfy the king's desires and secure his own position. The last thing he needed was the complication of tangled emotions.

In the quiet solitude of his study, he vowed to himself that he would keep his distance from Lottie, that he would quash any romantic notions that threatened to surface. He had come too far and worked too hard to let an attraction, no matter how undeniable, derail his ambitions.

With a renewed determination, he turned his attention back to the pages before him. There was a play to be written, a story to be told, and he couldn't afford to let anything—or anyone—stand in his way.

Thatcher couldn't remain still, and paced back and forth in his study, muttering to himself in frustration. "What a fool I am," he grumbled. "How could I let this happen?"

His ramblings grew increasingly agitated, and he couldn't contain the turmoil that churned within him. The image of Lottie, the fair maiden in his written scene, haunted his thoughts, and he couldn't escape the realization that he had unwittingly poured his desires onto the pages.

As he continued to berate himself, his voice grew louder, and the usually soundly sleeping Simms stirred in the adjoining room. With a groggy mumble, his servant shuffled into the study, blinking against the dim light of the low-burning lamp. "Is something amiss, sir?" the valet inquired.

Thatcher turned to him. "I can't believe I let this happen," he confessed, though it was more of a self-admonishment than an explanation.

The valet, having served Thatcher for years, was accustomed to his moments of restless agitation. He fetched a glass of water from a nearby table and offered it to his employer. "Perhaps a drink of water will help clear your mind, sir," he suggested.

Thatcher accepted the glass and took a long sip, the cool liquid momentarily soothing his frazzled nerves. He couldn't help but feel a pang of embarrassment at having his valet witness his inner turmoil. "Thank you, Simms," he said. "I apologize for disturbing your rest."

Simms, ever the loyal and understanding servant, shook his head. "No need for apologies, sir. It's my duty to attend to your needs, day or night."

Thatcher sighed, setting the glass aside. "I appreciate your loyalty. But I fear I've allowed myself to become entangled in a most unfortunate situation."

Simms, ever the patient listener, waited for his employer to continue.

"I've been writing romantic nonsense when I should be focused on our upcoming play for the king."

Simms raised an eyebrow, curious but not judgmental.

"And the worst part is," Thatcher continued, "I realized that

I've inadvertently penned a scene that...resembles someone I know."

Understanding dawned in Simms's eyes, and he offered a sympathetic nod. "Matters of the heart can be quite vexing, sir."

"Indeed. It's a distraction I can ill afford. I must remain focused on our work. The play demanded by King William."

Simms, ever the voice of reason, offered a reassuring smile. "You've always had a way of finding clarity in your writing. I have no doubt you'll overcome this."

But what if he didn't?

Thatcher nodded, appreciating his valet's unwavering support. "Thank you. Now, if you don't mind, I'll return to my writing. Perhaps the answer lies in the words themselves."

Simms returned to his room, leaving Thatcher alone in the dimly lit study. As he settled back at his desk, he was determined to regain control of his thoughts and emotions.

There was a play to be written, a story to be told, and he couldn't afford to let anything—or anyone—stand in his way.

Only...what if *he* stood in his way?

CHAPTER TEN

L OTTIE NAVIGATED THE bustling streets of London, her steps quick and determined as she made her way toward her sister-in-law Sadie's townhouse. The city was alive with activity, carriages rumbling past and vendors hawking their wares on street corners. Despite the ceaseless commotion, Lottie's thoughts were singularly focused on her mission.

She wished to interrogate her new sister.

Sadie had always fascinated Lottie with her unconventional story. A duchess who had once disguised herself as a male deal porter at the London Docks and found love in the most unexpected of places—it was a tale that intrigued and inspired her. She had often wondered how Sadie had navigated a man's world with such resilience and determination.

Upon reaching her sister-in-law's elegant townhouse in Mayfair, Lottie was greeted by the butler, a stately figure with a perfectly groomed mustache. "Lady Lottie," he greeted her with a nod. "The duchess is expecting you in the drawing room."

Lottie offered the butler a polite smile and followed him through the opulent halls of the townhouse. The interior was a testament to wealth and sophistication, with ornate furnishings and artwork that spoke of privilege and refinement.

Sadie awaited her in the drawing room, seated in a high-backed armchair with a book in hand. She looked every inch the duchess, her dark hair elegantly styled, her gown a marvel of silk and lace. But Lottie knew that beneath the veneer of aristocracy lay a woman who had faced her own trials and emerged stronger for it.

"Lottie," Sadie greeted her warmly, setting aside her book and rising to her feet. "It's a pleasure to see you again."

Lottie returned the smile and embraced Sadie. "The pleasure is mine," she replied. "I've been longing to hear more about your adventures as a deal porter. Every time we begin to converse on it, Crawford sticks his big nose in and demands to know the topic we discuss. It's rather infuriating."

Sadie led her to a cozy sitting area, and they settled in plush chairs, the scent of freshly brewed tea lingering in the air. "Ah, your brother. He doesn't like to discuss my days as a deal porter," Sadie mused. "It feels like a lifetime ago, truthfully, though the experiences are still vivid in my mind."

Lottie leaned forward, eager to hear more. "How did you manage it? To disguise yourself and work among the men?"

Sadie's expression turned thoughtful. "It wasn't easy, I'll admit," she began. "But necessity is a powerful motivator. I had no other choice if I wanted to survive on my own terms. I learned to blend in, to speak their language, and to work twice as hard to prove myself."

Lottie nodded. "And Crawford? How did he come into the knowledge of your deception?"

Sadie's eyes softened with affection as she spoke of her husband. "Crawford was a regular visitor at the docks, making excuses to personally check on the company's shipments," she explained, referring to Castlebury Shipping, the family business. "He saw through my disguise early on, but instead of exposing me, he helped me. He became my protector, my confidant, and, eventually, my love."

Lottie couldn't help but smile at the romantic twist in the tale. "It sounds like a true love story, against all odds."

Sadie chuckled, a hint of mischief in her eyes. "Indeed, it was. But love has a way of defying expectations, doesn't it?"

An image of Thatcher popped into Lottie's mind. She pushed it away, mortified.

Their conversation shifted to a more serious note as Sadie shared her experiences with the Revivalists, who had once posed a threat to her. "I faced my fair share of challenges," she admitted. "But surviving the Revivalists only made me more determined to live life on my own terms. I refuse to be a pawn in their games."

Lottie admired Sadie's resilience and determination. It was a lesson she hoped to carry with her as she navigated her own path in a society that often resisted change. "You've inspired me," she confessed. "Your strength and independence are something I greatly admire."

Sadie reached out to grasp her hand, the grip firm and reassuring. "Remember that you have the power to forge your own destiny," she said. "Don't let anyone else dictate the course of your life."

As Lottie left Sadie and Crawford's townhouse that day, she carried with her not only the wisdom of a duchess who had defied convention but also the knowledge that she, too, could face any challenge that lay ahead with determination and resilience. Sadie's story had lit a fire within her, igniting a renewed sense of purpose and the belief that she could make her mark on the world in her own unique way.

As she stepped out, a sense of exhilaration and independence coursed through her veins. She decided to take a leisurely walk through Hyde Park before returning to her own home a few streets over.

The short distance from Sadie's residence to the park's entrance gave her a few moments of solitude, a rare commodity for a woman of her station. Her heart swelled with appreciation for the simple beauty of the park. It was a stark contrast to the bustling streets of Mayfair, a reminder of the natural world that existed beyond the confines of Society. As she strolled along the winding path, she felt a sense of peace settle over her. She had always been drawn to the written word, finding solace and inspiration in the pages of books. Now, surrounded by the beauty of Hyde Park, she felt a connection to the world around her, a sense of belonging that went beyond the constraints of her gender and station.

However, her moment of serenity was shattered when she heard the approaching footsteps of a man behind her. She quickened her pace, her heart racing as she realized that she was alone in the park, vulnerable to the advances of a stranger.

The heavy footsteps drew closer, and Lottie's instincts screamed at her to flee. She didn't need to turn around to know that his intentions were far from honorable—she could *feel* it. Panic bubbled up inside her as she broke into a run, her skirts billowing around her.

The man's voice, oily and lecherous, reached her ears as he called out to her. "My sweet, there's no need to be so hasty. I only want to get to know you better."

Lottie's breath came in short, terrified gasps as she veered off the narrow path and into a dense thicket of trees. She knew that she couldn't outrun him, but she could try to lose him in the labyrinthine woods of the park. Branches and leaves scratched at her arms and face as she pushed through the undergrowth. Her heart pounded in her chest, and she prayed for a miracle to lead her to safety. She had heard stories of women who had fallen victim to men like this, and she refused to become another tragic tale.

The man's footsteps grew louder behind her, and Lottie knew that she was running out of time. She had to find a place to hide, to escape his clutches before it was too late. Finally, she spotted a large, gnarled tree with low-hanging branches. With a burst of desperation, she scrambled up into its leafy sanctuary, praying that the man wouldn't find her.

The world could be a perilous place for a woman, even in the most idyllic of settings.

Lottie clung to the branches, her breath coming in ragged gasps as she watched and waited. The man's voice drew ever nearer, his words filled with vile promises and threats.

"My sweet, don't be afraid," the man cooed, his voice dripping with malice. "I'll make it worth your while, I promise."

Lottie pressed a hand to her mouth to stifle a terrified sob. She couldn't respond to him, couldn't reveal her location.

"Come out, my poppet," he continued, his tone turning darker with impatience. "I won't hurt you. I just want to have a little fun."

The words sent a shiver down Lottie's spine, and she clung to the tree with all her strength. She knew that this man was dangerous, that he wouldn't hesitate to harm her if he found her.

"Just imagine the pleasures I can offer you," he purred, his footsteps growing closer to the tree. "You won't regret it, my lovely."

Lottie's heart pounded in her chest, and she prayed for a miracle to keep her hidden. She couldn't let this man touch her, couldn't allow herself to become another victim of his sinister desires. As the man continued his search below, Lottie remained frozen in place, her fingers trembling on the tree branches. She knew that she had to wait, to let him grow frustrated and leave. Only then could she safely make her way back to the safety of her own townhouse.

The man continued to call out, his tone increasingly desperate as he realized he couldn't find Lottie. He stomped around the base of the tree, cursing under his breath, the words becoming more and more incomprehensible as his anger grew.

"Come out, you wretched girl!" he shouted, his voice cracking with frustration. "I know you're here somewhere. You can't hide from me forever!"

Lottie held her breath. She knew that any movement or sound could give her away. The man's threats and insults continued, but Lottie remained hidden, determined not to reveal herself.

Finally, after what felt like an eternity, the man let out a roar of frustration that echoed through the woods. It was a chilling sound, and Lottie shivered as she listened. "Damn you, girl!" he yelled one last time, his voice filled with anger and defeat. And with that, his heavy footsteps receded into the distance, growing fainter and fainter until they were but a distant memory.

Lottie waited a few moments longer, trembling with a mix of fear and relief. She knew that she had narrowly escaped a dangerous situation, and she was acutely aware of how vulnerable women like her were in a world filled with predatory men. She allowed herself to hope that he had given up the search and left Hyde Park. She cautiously began to ease herself down from the tree, but suddenly, the sound of his re-approaching steps made her heart leap into her throat.

He returned, his face twisted in a cruel grin that sent a shiver down Lottie's spine. He loomed at the base of the tree, his voice dripping with malice. "You'll regret this, girl," he sneered, his eyes filled with a menacing glint. "When I tell my brothers what you did, they'll make sure you pay for your insolence."

Lottie's fear deepened. She had no idea who this man's brothers were or what they were capable of, but the ominous threat hung heavily in the air. She knew she had to get away from him, and fast.

With one final, chilling laugh, the man turned and disappeared for good into the night, leaving Lottie trembling in the tree, her heart pounding with fear. She waited until she was absolutely certain he was gone before cautiously descending from her hiding place. With trembling hands, she straightened her clothing and smoothed her hair, attempting to regain her composure. Quickly, she made it to the entrance of the park.

Spotting a hackney carriage nearby, she rushed toward it. "Rhodes Theatre!" Lottie implored the driver with a quiver in her voice as she flung open the carriage door and leaped inside. Her urgency left no room for argument, and the driver spurred the horses into action.

As the carriage clattered through the dimly lit streets of London, Lottie's mind raced with questions. Who was that man, and why had he pursued her with such sinister intent? The night had taken a terrifying turn, and she couldn't shake the feeling that danger still lurked in the shadows, ready to strike when she least expected.

⤜⟫⟫⟫⟪⟪⟪⤛

LOTTIE STEPPED INTO Rhodes Theatre with her heart still racing from her terrifying encounter. She hadn't expected to find herself there at this late hour, but the need for a place of refuge had driven her to seek solace in familiar surroundings. To her surprise, she walked right into a flurry of activity on the stage. Actors moved about, rehearsing their lines and blocking out scenes.

And at the center of it all stood Thatcher, taking charge and directing them through the first rough scene of the play they had been working on together.

She watched him with a mix of fascination and frustration. His commanding presence was undeniable, and it was clear that the actors respected his authority. But as she observed the scene unfolding before her, a critical eye couldn't help but find fault.

Thatcher paced back and forth, offering instructions and corrections, and Lottie couldn't resist speaking her mind. "No, no, no," she muttered to herself, her lips curling into a bemused smile. A nearby stagehand glanced at her curiously, but Lottie ignored the scrutiny. She was too engrossed in what was happening on stage.

Thatcher paused, his gaze shifting toward her, and their eyes locked for a brief moment. Lottie could see the flicker of surprise, and she raised an eyebrow. "What's wrong with the scene?" he asked, his tone carrying a hint of amusement.

Lottie couldn't hold back any longer. "Everything," she replied bluntly, her voice carrying across the stage. "The pacing is all wrong, and the actors lack chemistry. It's as if they're reciting lines from a script rather than embodying their characters."

A murmur of agreement rippled through the actors, and Thatcher shot her a tight smile. "Well, Lady Lottie, it seems you have a keen eye for the theatre," he remarked, not sounding the least bit happy about it. "Perhaps you'd like to enlighten us with your expertise another time."

Lottie stepped onto the stage, her confidence bolstered by the challenge. "Now seems the perfect time," she countered, her voice ringing with authority.

CHAPTER ELEVEN

T HATCHER STOOD AT the center of the stage as he directed the actors through their scenes. He had a clear vision of how the play should unfold, and he intended to see it realized. But as he spoke, offering instructions and guidance, he felt a pair of intense blue eyes boring into him.

Lottie had arrived at the theatre unannounced, and from the moment she had laid eyes on the rehearsal, it was evident that she was far from pleased with his direction. She stood off to the side, her arms crossed over her chest, her expression one of disapproval.

The tension in the air was palpable as Thatcher's patience began to wane. He watched as Lottie stepped onto the stage, her determination clear. "Stop!" she exclaimed, her voice cutting through the room.

The actors froze, looking between Thatcher and Lottie with a mix of confusion and curiosity.

Lottie marched up to one of the actors, a tall man with a quiet demeanor. "You, sir, are playing your part all wrong," she declared.

Thatcher's jaw clenched as he resisted the urge to interrupt. He knew that this collaboration wouldn't be easy, but he hadn't expected Lottie to be quite so...assertive.

The actor, unsure of whose direction to follow, exchanged a bewildered glance with Thatcher. "Um..."

Lottie turned to the rest of the cast. "And you, you should be emphasizing the subtext in this scene, not glossing over it like a schoolboy reciting his lessons."

Thatcher had had enough. "Lady Lottie, I appreciate your input, but I am directing this play," he stated firmly.

Lottie spun to face him, her eyes flashing with defiance. "Your direction is leading this play into mediocrity," she retorted, her voice dripping with disdain.

"I beg your pardon?"

"You heard me, you overinflated scribbler."

"What did you call me?" A *scribbler?* "Oh, I beg to differ," Thatcher growled, ready to do battle over that insult.

Their exchange grew heated, and the actors watched in stunned silence. Rainville, drawn from his office by the commotion, observed the scene with a raised eyebrow. "Is there a problem here?" he loudly inquired.

Thatcher and Lottie both turned to him, their faces flushed with anger and frustration. "No problem at all," Thatcher replied, his tone laced with forced civility.

"Absolutely none," Lottie agreed, her voice tight with indignation.

The actors exchanged knowing glances and stifled chuckles at the obvious tension between the two.

Rainville, however, was not so easily fooled. He regarded them both with a shrewd expression. "It's clear to anyone with eyes that there's something more than just creative differences between the two of you," he remarked with a smug, knowing smile.

Thatcher was instantly appalled, his protests of innocence quick and vehement. "Nonsense," he scoffed.

"Utter nonsense," Lottie echoed.

Rainville chuckled, seemingly entertained by their denial. "Well, then," he said. "Let's get back to work, shall we?"

Thatcher quietly stormed off the stage, his frustration evident in every step. Lottie followed closely behind. "This discussion is far from over, Mr. Goodrich."

Their fire had only just begun, and the undeniable chemistry between them simmered beneath the surface, waiting to ignite. He felt it, try as he did to ignore it.

Thatcher seethed as he walked. Lottie's determined steps echoed in the corridor as she kept pace with him. As they moved away from the prying eyes and ears of the actors, he experienced a strange mixture of irritation and attraction toward Lottie. She was infuriatingly opinionated, but her passion for their project was undeniable. Despite their many disagreements, he couldn't deny that there was something intriguing about her.

They entered a narrow hallway, the walls adorned with faded posters from past productions. Thatcher stopped abruptly, turning to face her. "Lady Lottie," he began, his voice low and controlled, "I understand that you have your own ideas about the play, but I must insist that I am the director, and my decisions are final."

Lottie met his gaze head-on. "I don't doubt your abilities," she replied, equally determined. "But I also won't stand by and watch this play become a mediocre production when I know it could be so much more."

Thatcher clenched his fists at his sides, torn between frustration and admiration for her tenacity. "I am not averse to constructive criticism," he admitted, though it grated on his ego to say so. "But there is a way to go about it, and your approach lacks all finesse."

Lottie raised an eyebrow, unimpressed by his condescension. "Perhaps you could use a bit more humility, *Mr. Goodrich.*"

Their gazes locked, sparks of tension and attraction dancing between them. Thatcher was acutely aware of her proximity, the heat of her breath against his lips. He closed his eyes tight, ready to dismiss her and seek some space away from her before he did something he shouldn't. Like kiss her again.

"Thatcher, I demand that you listen to me!"

"What is it, Lady Lottie?" He couldn't hide the exasperation in his voice as he opened his eyes and focused on her.

Her cheeks were flushed, and her eyes sparked with anger. "You can't just dismiss my opinions. This play is as much mine as it is yours."

Thatcher's temper suddenly flared, and he found himself unable to hold back. "You think because you had one good idea, you're suddenly an expert on playwriting?"

Lottie bristled at his condescension. "I know talent when I see it, Mr. Goodrich. And I know you're afraid that my talent might overshadow yours."

His jaw tightened as he stared her down. "You're delusional."

"Am I? Or are you just too proud to admit that you might not be the best playwright in London anymore?"

Thatcher's frustration reached its breaking point, and he let out an exasperated sigh. "This is pointless. We'll never agree."

Just as it seemed their argument might escalate into something else entirely, a sudden clearing of a throat interrupted them. They both turned to find Rainville standing there, an unholy glint in his eyes. "I must say, the two of you make quite the pair," the duke remarked.

Thatcher took a step back from Lottie, their fiery interlude momentarily forgotten in the presence of their employer.

Rainville continued, his tone more serious now. "But let us not forget the task at hand. We have a play to perfect for the king, and I have every confidence that the two of you will find a way to work together."

Thatcher flicked a glance toward Lottie. They might not like each other very much at the moment, he realized, but they both had too much at stake to let their differences derail their shared endeavor.

"If you'll excuse me." He turned on his heel and strode down the hallway before he said anything more he might regret.

⇥⟫⟩⟨⟨⟨⟵

LOTTIE STORMED INTO Thatcher's makeshift office in the theatre, her face flushed with anger and determination. Clearly, she had no intention of letting him evade another argument any longer.

Thatcher, who had been meticulously arranging some scripts on a cluttered table, looked up in surprise as she entered. "Lady Lottie, what is it now?" His tone dripped with impatience.

"What is it *now*?" Lottie echoed. "It's you, Mr. Goodrich. It's your stubbornness and arrogance!"

Thatcher clenched his jaw. "I could say the same about you."

Their argument morphed into a sharp exchange of words that echoed through the small, candlelit room. They clashed over every aspect of the play, from character motivations to plot development. He wasn't willing to give an inch, and neither was she, and his frustration grew with each passing moment.

Her cheeks were flushed with anger, and her blue eyes blazed with intensity as she accused him of being close-minded and dismissive of her ideas. Thatcher, equally frustrated, retorted with biting remarks about her inexperience and her audacity to question his expertise. "You think because you're allowed to pair with me in this creative endeavor that it at all provides liberty for you to profess opinions far above your knowledge and experience. Well, I am here to assure you that it does not."

But beneath the heated argument, there was something else, something neither of them wanted to admit. The chemistry between them crackled like electricity, an undeniable attraction that defied reason. As their voices grew louder, their faces drew closer, and in a moment of heated tension, their lips crashed together in a searing kiss.

The world seemed to disappear as Thatcher kissed her, the room around him fading into oblivion. It was a kiss fueled by frustration and desire, a kiss that ignited a passion neither of them had anticipated. Their hands clung to each other, fingers tangling in hair and fabric as she pressed her body boldly to his, and for that fleeting moment, all his doubts and arguments vanished.

But as quickly as the kiss had begun, it ended, leaving

Thatcher breathless and bewildered. He pulled away, his eyes locked with hers in a stunned silence, the unspoken tension between them heavy in the air.

Lottie's lips parted from his in a startled gasp, her breaths coming fast and shallow. She stumbled backward, her voice slightly shaky as she stammered, "I... I... That was..." Her words trailed off into an awkward silence as she attempted to regain her composure.

His heart still pounded in his chest. He was frazzled and flustered, his thoughts scattered like leaves in the wind.

"I... I'm sorry," Lottie finally managed, her voice a bit more composed. "I shouldn't have—"

But before she could finish her sentence, Thatcher cut her off, his voice filled with forced casualness. "No need to apologize, Lady Lottie." Why was he being so flippant?

⋙⋘

LOTTIE FELT HER heart sink at the abrupt change in his demeanor. She had hoped that their passionate encounter would bring them closer, but it seemed to have had the opposite effect, pushing him further away. She swallowed hard, trying to shake off the embarrassment and confusion that clouded her thoughts.

Thatcher leaned casually against the cluttered desk, watching Lottie with an infuriatingly smug expression. His lips curled into a self-satisfied smirk, and there was a glint of amusement in his eyes. He seemed entirely unaffected by their passionate kiss, as though it had meant nothing to him.

Lottie felt her anger flare as she met his gaze. "Is that all you have to say?" she demanded. "You kiss me like that, and now you're acting as if it never happened?"

Thatcher chuckled, a low, maddeningly nonchalant sound. "Why, Lady Lottie, it was just a kiss," he replied. "Surely you're not one to make a fuss over such trivial matters."

Her jaw tightened as she clenched her fists, struggling to contain her rising anger. "Trivial?" Lottie retorted, her voice trembling with a mix of hurt and indignation. "You are insufferable, Mr. Goodrich. You kiss me and then dismiss it as if it means nothing."

He pushed away from the desk and approached her slowly, his every step oozing a maddening confidence. "Perhaps it doesn't mean anything," he murmured, his voice low and provocative. "Or perhaps I simply have other priorities."

Lottie's frustration boiled over, and she couldn't stand the way he was toying with her emotions. "Other *priorities?*" she spat. "I should have known better than to expect anything more from a man like you!" With a sharp turn, Lottie spun on her heel and marched toward the door, determined to put as much distance between herself and Thatcher as possible. She couldn't let him see just how deeply his cavalier attitude had wounded her pride. As she flung open the door and stormed out of his office, she could still hear his infuriating laughter echoing in the corridor behind her, a mocking reminder of their fiery encounter and the undeniable attraction that simmered between them.

Lottie's departure from Rhodes Theatre left her feeling anxious and unsettled. As she stepped out onto the London streets, her thoughts turned to the menacing man she had encountered in Hyde Park. The mention of his "brothers" had sent a chill down her spine. What if he was connected to the Revivalists, the notorious group of noblemen who had a reputation for violence and intimidation?

She muttered to herself in frustration as she walked briskly. "Revivalists, indeed. As if I don't have enough to worry about." The gas lamps cast eerie, flickering shadows on the cobblestone streets, and her imagination began to run wild. She knew all too well the stories of the Revivalists' ruthless tactics and their disdain for those who dared to challenge the status quo. If they ever discovered that she was the true author behind Goodrich's last play, they'd undoubtedly come after her. For challenge the status quo she most certainly had.

Lost in her thoughts, she decided that walking alone through the dark streets was unwise. It was then that she spotted a lone hackney carriage approaching. With a sigh of relief, Lottie raised her hand to flag down the driver.

The carriage pulled to a stop, and the driver leaned over, casting a curious glance her way. He was a middle-aged man with a weathered face. "Oy! Where to, miss?" he asked, his voice gruff but not unkind.

She hesitated for a moment, not wanting to reveal her true destination in case she was being followed. "Just...drive," she replied vaguely.

The hackney driver raised an eyebrow but didn't press further. He nodded and gestured for her to get in. As she settled into the aged carriage, Lottie felt a sense of unease. The creaking of the wheels and the rhythmic clip-clop of the horse's hooves on the cobblestones seemed to echo her own racing heartbeat. She glanced out the small window, watching the city pass by in a blur of shadows and lamplight. Her thoughts drifted back to the lecher in the park, the Revivalists, and the dangers that might await her. It was clear that she needed to be cautious every moment.

Such was a lady's life.

CHAPTER TWELVE

T HATCHER'S HEART RACED as he followed the palace servant through the grand corridors of King William IV's residence. He had been summoned to discuss the progress of the play, and the thought of meeting the king in person filled him with a mixture of awe and trepidation. He felt the weight of the occasion, knowing that the success of his and Lottie's play could have far-reaching consequences.

Beside him, Lottie walked with a determined stride, her presence a reassuring anchor in the sea of uncertainty. She had insisted on accompanying him to the meeting, refusing to let Thatcher meet the king alone. Lottie wanted to ensure that Thatcher didn't say or do anything that might jeopardize their collaborative efforts.

The palace itself was a marvel of opulence, with gilded walls and crystal chandeliers. The air was scented with the fragrant blooms of the autumn garden, and the distant sound of a piano playing a delicate melody wafted through the air. Thatcher couldn't help but marvel at the grandeur of it all, though he was acutely aware that he was far removed from the impoverished artist's life he had once led.

As they entered a lavish drawing room, King William himself was seated at a tea table near a large window that overlooked the garden. The king, a portly man with a hearty laugh and a twinkle in his blue eyes, greeted them warmly. "Good afternoon, Mr.

Goodrich," he said as he extended his hand for Thatcher to shake. "And who is this lovely lady accompanying you today?"

"Your Majesty, may I present Lady Lottie Castlebury, a dear friend and a passionate supporter of the arts. She shares my enthusiasm for the theatre."

He watched Lottie execute a graceful curtsy, her gaze steady and respectful as she addressed the king. "Your Majesty, it is an honor to be in your presence. I've long admired your support for the arts and your dedication to our beloved country."

The king beamed with delight at the compliment, and they were invited to join him at the tea table. Biscuits and freshly brewed tea were served, and the conversation turned to the progress of their play.

Thatcher exchanged a quick, nervous glance with Lottie, and her own unease was apparent. But he took a deep breath and began to discuss their work with the king, describing the themes and characters they had developed, and the central conflict that would drive the narrative. As he spoke, the king listened attentively, occasionally nodding or asking insightful questions. His friendly demeanor put Thatcher somewhat at ease, but the weight of the situation was still palpable.

When he had finished the presentation, the king leaned back in his chair and regarded them both with a thoughtful expression. "I must say, Mr. Goodrich and Lady Lottie, I am quite intrigued by this play. It sounds like a story that the audience will find most captivating. Myself most especially."

Relief swept through Thatcher, and he glanced at Lottie once more, his tension dissipating slightly. It seemed that his presentation had met with the king's approval. "Thank you, Your Majesty," he replied, his throat dry as sand. "I am honored by your interest and continued support."

The king raised his teacup in a toast. "To the theatre and the arts!" he declared, and they clinked their teacups together.

As they continued to discuss the play and their plans for its production, Thatcher couldn't help but marvel at the odd turn of events. He had come a long way from the struggling playwright he once was, and now he found himself in the presence of the king, with Lady Lottie by his side—the most infuriating, damnably beautiful, and exceedingly talented woman he'd ever met.

As King William reminisced about the theatre, his mind turned to his once-beloved Dorothea, Thatcher felt a mixture of fascination and trepidation. The king's voice carried a wistful tone as he spoke of the actress who had long ago captured his heart and given him several children. "Ah, Dotti," he sighed, his eyes distant. "She was a remarkable woman, a brilliant actress, and the mother of my children. We had our share of joys and sorrows, but I will always cherish the memories we created together."

Lottie leaned forward, her eyes shining with admiration. "Your Majesty, I've always been inspired by Ms. Jordan's talent and strength," she confessed. "She paved the way for many women in the theatre, proving that they could command the stage as well as any man."

"You, Lady Lottie, remind me of her in many ways," he said, his voice tinged with nostalgia. "The same fire, the same determination to excel in a world that often underestimates women. Dotti would have been proud of your achievements."

Thatcher watched the exchange, aware of the significance of the king's words. Lottie, with her passion for the theatre and her unwavering determination, was being compared to the famous actress who had once captured the heart of a king, Jane Austen herself, and the whole of London. He couldn't deny the admiration and attraction he felt for Lottie in that moment, even as it stoked the embers of their complicated relationship.

Her fiery spirit had always intrigued him, but now, in the presence of the king's praise, he felt something more. It was a stirring deep within his chest, an unsettling sensation he couldn't quite name. He glanced away, hoping to conceal the turmoil in his eyes. This wasn't the plan! He had never intended to become so entangled with Lady Lottie, and yet here they were. It was a situation he couldn't have foreseen, and it left him feeling vulnerable in ways he didn't want to admit. Thatcher had always been the master of his own fate, relying on his sharp wit and determination to carve a path to success. But with Lottie by his side, challenging him at every turn and stoking unfamiliar feelings, he couldn't help but feel like a man teetering on the edge of something unknown and dangerous. And he didn't like it one bit.

Amidst the king's conversation, Thatcher suddenly heard a distant bark, followed by a servant's frantic shout in the background. He turned his attention toward the commotion and couldn't suppress a grin as he spotted an exuberant Irish setter sprinting toward them.

"Oh dear!" the servant cried, trying to catch up with the canine whirlwind. "Forgive me, Your Majesty. Monty's gotten away again!"

Thatcher chuckled, his gaze fixed on the approaching dog. "Well, I suppose he's eager to join our discussion, Your Majesty," he quipped.

King William's eyes widened as the dog drew nearer, his once-regal countenance breaking into a bemused smile. "It seems that Monty has his own opinions about the matters at hand," he observed.

As the setter bounded toward them, Thatcher leaned down, extending a hand in greeting. "Hello, Monty," he said with a grin, ruffling the dog's fur. Monty responded with enthusiastic wagging and an attempt to shower Thatcher with slobbery kisses.

The servant finally managed to catch up. "I'm so sorry, Your Majesty," he panted, his face flushed with embarrassment.

The king waved off the apology with a good-natured chuckle. "No harm done, I think Monty has made his point," he remarked, casting a playful glance at Thatcher. "He's clearly a fan of our discussions."

Thatcher straightened once more and listened with rapt attention as King William again expressed his anticipation for the upcoming play. "I must confess, Mr. Goodrich, I am quite eager to witness the magic you shall create on the stage. It's been far too long since I've had the pleasure of attending a truly exceptional theatrical performance. Why, the last time was your last play!"

Thatcher felt a mixture of pride and pressure at the king's words. His play was expected to deliver, and the weight of anticipation hung heavily in the air.

Lottie, always quick with words, responded with a charming smile. "Your Majesty, we are deeply honored by your enthusiasm and support," she said. "Rest assured, Mr. Goodrich shall put his heart and soul into this production, aiming to create a play that will captivate and delight you."

The king nodded appreciatively. "I have no doubt that he shall, Lady Lottie," he replied. "The stage has a way of bringing forth extraordinary talent, and I have the utmost confidence in his abilities."

As the king continued to express his excitement and offer anecdotes about his past experiences in the theatre, Thatcher remained filled with both apprehension and determination. The King's approval was a powerful motivator, but it also meant that his—well, *their*—work would be under close scrutiny. They couldn't afford to disappoint.

A pang of guilt tugged at his conscience. He knew, as well as Lottie did, that she was every bit as responsible for the play's creation as he was. Her insights, ideas, and passion had breathed life into their collaborative effort. But he also understood the harsh realities of the world they lived in. Women faced numerous restrictions and prejudices when it came to the arts, especially in the realm of playwriting. The theatre world was male-dominated, and it was a realm where women often struggled to gain recognition for their talents. Thatcher admired Lottie's determination and skill, but he couldn't openly acknowledge her contributions without risking her reputation and future prospects in the theatre.

The weight of this unspoken truth bore down on him as King William praised his work. While he felt pride in the collaboration, there was also a sense of unease, knowing that Lottie's role in their success would remain hidden. It was a silent compromise they had made, one born out of necessity rather than desire.

And, for now, that would have to be enough.

CHAPTER THIRTEEN

T HATCHER SAT AT the worn wooden counter of the Meadow-lark Tavern, nursing his drink as he stewed over the turmoil in his heart. The rustic establishment was a haven for those seeking solace in spirits, its atmosphere a blend of camaraderie and anonymity. The lanterns cast dancing shadows across the worn tables and the cracked leather seats.

West, the American bartender with a penchant for mixing strong concoctions, leaned against the bar, a sympathetic ear to the troubles of the patrons. He had become something of a confidant to Thatcher, who found himself there wrestling with his internal conflicts.

With a heavy sigh, Thatcher grumbled, "She's infuriating. Absolutely bloody infuriating." He swirled the amber liquid in his snifter, clinking the ice cubes softly.

West, big and burly, shot him a knowing look. "Ah, a lady, eh? That's who's got you all twisted up inside?"

Thatcher nodded, his scowl deepening. "Exactly. She's got this uncanny ability to get under my skin, challenge everything I do, and yet…" He paused, searching for the right words. "And yet I can't deny the attraction. It's like she's a walking contradiction, like she counters everything I am and do, and it's driving me mad."

West chuckled, pouring himself a shot of bourbon. "Love and attraction have a way of making a man's life more interesting, my friend."

Thatcher scoffed. "Love? Don't be absurd. It's nothing of the sort. It's just…" He struggled to articulate his feelings. "It's just that she's talented, smart, and she won't let anyone tell her otherwise. It's maddening."

West raised an eyebrow. "Sounds like someone's hooked good."

Thatcher scowled even deeper, if that were possible. "Hooked? Hardly. This isn't a romantic novel, man. It's real life, and I've got enough on my plate without adding the complications of a woman like Lady Lottie."

The bartender chuckled again, taking a sip of his drink. "Well, you've got a choice, I reckon. You can keep stewing in here, or you can face those feelings head-on."

Thatcher grunted in response, finishing his drink in one swift gulp. "I'll take another. And make it a strong one."

As West began to prepare another drink, he shook his head. "Love or not, it seems you're in for a tumultuous ride, if Lady Lottie Castlebury's at the center of it all."

"Well I know it," Thatcher groused.

"Look," West began, his voice carrying a tone of somber reflection, "once upon a time, there was a man who thought he'd found the love of his life." He poured himself another glass of bourbon, his expression distant.

Thatcher raised an eyebrow, intrigued by the sudden change in West's demeanor. "Go on."

The bartender's eyes seemed to focus on a distant memory as he continued, "This man had met a woman who was everything he'd ever dreamed of—beautiful, vivacious, and full of life. She had a way of making every day feel like an adventure. They were inseparable."

Thatcher listened intently, the weight of his own troubles momentarily pushed aside by West's tale.

"But as they say, all good things must come to an end," West continued, his voice tinged with sadness. "You see, this woman had a secret, a dark one that she kept hidden. She was a gambler, addicted to the thrill of risking it all. And, well, the man loved her enough to trust her, even when he shouldn't have."

Thatcher frowned, sensing the impending tragedy of the story.

"One day," West continued, "she asked him for a large sum of money to settle a debt. She swore it was the last time, and, being madly in love, he gave her every penny he had saved."

Thatcher winced, recognizing the all-too-familiar theme of betrayal and heartbreak.

West raised his glass, as if to toast to lost love. "And you know what happened? She took the money and disappeared, leaving him with nothing but shattered dreams and a broken heart."

Thatcher's heart ached for the bartender. "I'm sorry, mate," he said softly.

West smiled, but it was a bittersweet smile that held the weight of years of regret. "Don't be. It's a lesson learned the hard way. The heart has a way of healing, even when it's broken."

Thatcher thought of Lottie and the tangled mess of emotions she stirred within him. Perhaps there was a lesson to be learned from West's story—to be cautious with matters of the heart, even when faced with undeniable attraction. As he sipped his drink and contemplated his own feelings, Thatcher couldn't help but wonder if Lottie would be the one to heal or break his heart.

Thatcher leaned in closer across the bar top, his eyes clouded with introspection. "West, have you ever done something you felt guilty about later? Something that nags at you, day in and day out?"

West nodded slowly. "We've all got our demons. Guilt can be a powerful force, eating away at you if you let it."

Thatcher sighed, running a hand through his hair in frustration. "I've taken something that doesn't rightfully belong to me. I can't shake the feeling that I'm in the wrong."

"Regret's a heavy burden to carry. The question is, what are you going to do about it?"

Thatcher looked at his glass, lost in thought. "I don't know. I don't know."

He nursed his ale as he mulled over the events of the day, thoughts of Lottie lingering in his mind, her presence like a melody that refused to fade away.

Lost in his reverie, he barely noticed when a hand clapped him on the shoulder.

"Thatcher, old chap, fancy a game of cards?" came a familiar, good-natured voice from behind him.

Startled, Thatcher turned to see Edward Waverly grinning at him, an amused look in his eye. He hesitated for a moment, torn between the comfort of his solitude and the prospect of some much-needed distraction. But then he caught sight of the eager gleam in the actor's eye, and he found himself nodding in agreement. "Why not?" he replied with a wry smile, pushing aside his half-empty glass. "Lead the way."

With a boisterous laugh, Edward led Thatcher through the crowded tavern to a back table where a group of their fellow actors had gathered for a friendly game of cards. The air was thick with the smell of tobacco and ale, the lively chatter of patrons a buzzing backdrop to the clinking of glasses and the shuffle of cards.

"Good of you to join us."

"Goodrich!"

"Pull up a chair. David's dealing."

"Let's see how you do with numbers instead of words, playwright."

Thatcher settled into his seat at the table, the familiar sound of laughter washing over him like a comforting wave. It had been too long since he'd indulged in such simple pleasures, too long since he'd allowed himself to be swept up in the easy banter of friends. "Deal me in."

As the game progressed, he lost track of time, his worries and cares fading into the background as he focused on the cards before him. The tension of the day melted away, replaced by a sense of ease that he had sorely missed. And as he glanced around the table at his fellow actors, their faces lit up with smiles and laughter, Thatcher couldn't help but feel a sense of gratitude for the moment.

As the cards were shuffled and hands were dealt, the conversation turned to more lighthearted topics, and Thatcher's mind wandered as his friends began to gossip about their women.

"I tell you, boys, my missus has been on my case about painting the blasted kitchen for weeks now," one of the actors exclaimed with a hearty laugh. "I swear, if I have to hear one more word about the color of the bloody walls, I'll—"

His words were cut off by a chorus of laughter from the table, the men nodding in understanding as they commiserated with his plight.

"My wife wants another babe."

"Mine says I need to earn more and drink less."

"That's nothing. My wife threatened to move her sister in with us—and she has eight children!"

"If it weren't for the gift between their legs, we'd not put up with them, eh?"

Thatcher tried to join in by forcing a chuckle, but his mind kept drifting back to Lottie. He couldn't help but picture her sitting beside him, her own laughter ringing sweetly in his ears.

Try as he might to push the thoughts aside, Lottie remained ever-present, her image haunting him like a persistent, beautiful ghost.

As the night wore on and the ale flowed freely, Thatcher found himself longing for the quiet solitude of his own company. With a muttered excuse, he rose from the table, bidding his friends a hasty farewell. "Until the morrow, good men."

With that, he left the Meadowlark Tavern behind, a cloud of thoughts swirling in his head, his pace unsteady as he navigated Covent Garden. His thoughts weighed heavily on him, making every step feel burdensome. He knew he needed some fresh air, some space to clear his mind. The night air was cool, carrying with it the scents of roasted chestnuts, ale, and damp cobblestones.

He was so lost in his thoughts that he hardly noticed the dark figures that had been following him.

Suddenly, they closed in, their footsteps falling in menacing unison. Thatcher turned to face them, his heart pounding in his chest. They were a group of rough-looking men, their faces obscured by shadows and the brims of their hats pulled low. "What do you want?" he demanded, his voice trembling with fear and anger.

One of the men stepped forward, a sinister grin stretching across his face. "We heard you've been working on a little project for the king, playwright," he sneered. "We want to know what that's all about. Because we don't like what you had to say in the last one. Not one bit."

"You made some of us look rather bad, chum."

"Aye, described us in bleak terms, chap."

"We don't take well to such slights. I'm afraid you'll have to pay a hefty price."

What slight? Who had he described in bleak terms?

The answer came swift and hard. *Noblemen.* He'd taken a hard swipe at noblemen.

Thatcher felt a sinking sensation in his gut. He had no idea who these men were, but their intentions couldn't be good. He considered making a run for it, but they had him surrounded, and the alley was narrow and dark. Before he could react, they descended upon him like a pack of wolves, fists flying and boots striking. The blows rained down on him from all sides, and he could do nothing but try to protect his head and torso as best he could.

Minutes stretched into an eternity as the merciless assault continued. Thatcher's vision blurred, and he felt blood trickling from a split lip and a throbbing pain in his ribs. He could barely hear their taunts and jeers through the ringing in his ears. Just when he thought he couldn't take any more, the attack abruptly stopped.

"We said we wouldn't kill him, lads. We promised to leave the playwright alive for him. Let's go break some windows." The men, satisfied with their brutality, stepped back, leaving Thatcher battered and gasping for breath on the cold cobblestones.

Gritting his teeth against the pain, he managed to pull himself to his feet, swaying unsteadily. Blood dripped from his battered face as he staggered in the direction of the nearest refuge he could think of—Aaron Longfellow's boxing gym.

⟩⟩⟩✶⟨⟨⟨

THE GYM WAS a cavernous brick and stone space filled with the rhythmic sounds of fists striking leather bags and the heavy thud of boxing gloves connecting with flesh. At the center of it all, in the ring, stood Aaron, the giant man with fiery auburn hair.

Thatcher stumbled through the gym's entrance, his vision hazy, and his legs barely carrying him. He managed to gasp out, "Longfellow, please... Take me home."

The boxer, seeing the sorry state of Thatcher, immediately rushed to his side. "What bloody happened to you, eh?" He slung Thatcher's arm around his shoulder and guided him toward the gym's exit. The other boxers paused in their training to watch, some offering silent nods of acknowledgment.

As they left the gym, Thatcher's world began to spin, and he could feel consciousness slipping away. With Aaron's support, he clung to the faint glimmer of awareness he had left, determined to make it home.

But determination only got one so far.

As the cold night air washed over him, Thatcher's strength gave out, and he passed out in Aaron's arms.

With Thatcher's weight heavy on the boxer's shoulders, Aaron trudged through the deserted streets of London, the rhythmic thud of their footsteps echoing in the silence of the night. The air was thick with tension and worry as they approached Thatcher's townhouse, its once-imposing façade looming in the darkness.

With a mighty grunt, Aaron guided Thatcher up the steps to the front door, his breath coming in ragged gasps as he pounded on the solid wood with his free hand. "Simms! Open up, damn it!" he shouted, his voice echoing in the stillness of the night.

As the door swung open, Simms's eyes widened in shock at the sight before him. "What in blazes happened?" he exclaimed, his voice tinged with worry as he rushed forward to assist Aaron in carrying Thatcher inside.

"There's no time for questions now," Aaron replied tersely, his voice strained with effort as they carefully navigated their way through the dimly lit foyer. "We need to get him cleaned up and tended to, and quickly."

The men maneuvered Thatcher into the nearest sitting room, laying him gently on the plush, frayed sofa as they worked to assess the extent of his injuries. As he gradually regained full consciousness, the world around him slowly came back into focus. The soft lamplight illuminated the familiar surroundings of his sitting room, casting a warm glow over the worried faces of Aaron and Simms as they hovered over him.

With a groan, Thatcher attempted to sit up, his head pounding with each movement. He dropped back down.

Simms wasted no time in pressing him for answers. "What in heaven's name happened, sir?" his valet demanded, fixing Thatcher with a stern gaze.

Thatcher winced at the sharpness of Simms's tone, the memories of the night's events blurry. He struggled to find the words to explain, his thoughts still muddled from the effects of the alcohol and the blow to his head. "I...I'm not entirely sure," he admitted, his voice hoarse with exhaustion. "I remember...the tavern, and then...everything went black."

The boxer exchanged a worried glance with the valet. It was

clear that something serious had occurred.

"Well, whatever happened, sir, we'll get to the bottom of it," Simms declared with determination. "But for now, you need to rest and regain your strength. We'll take care of everything else."

With gentle hands, Simms and Aaron helped Thatcher settle back onto the sofa, arranging pillows and blankets around him to ensure his comfort. As exhaustion threatened to pull him back into the darkness of unconsciousness, he suddenly remembered something with a flash of agonizing pain in his head. "I remember ..." he began, his voice strained with effort as he struggled to piece together the fragments now flying through his memory. "I was leaving the tavern when...someone attacked me."

Simms's eyes widened. "Attacked? By whom?"

Thatcher gently shook his head, the details of the attack still hazy in his aching mind. "I'm not sure... It happened so fast. But whoever it was, they meant to do me harm."

He saw Aaron's jaw clench with anger. "We need to report this to the authorities," the boxer said. "No one gets away with attacking one of our own."

Thatcher nodded in agreement, and immediately regretted the movement. "Yes, we must. But first, I need to gather my wits and make sense of what happened." As his memory sharpened, he recalled the distinct sound of the attackers' voices, the refined accents that hinted at upper-class breeding. It sent a chill down his spine as he pieced together the events of the night. "It was them," he murmured. "The Revivalists."

Simms and Aaron exchanged troubled glances. They all knew too well the dangerous nature of the group and the havoc they wreaked on those who challenged their beliefs.

"The bloody hell are they up to with you?" Aaron muttered, his fists clenched at his sides in frustration.

Thatcher's mind raced with the implications of the Revivalists' involvement. He remembered their heated words, their threats of retribution against those who dared to oppose them. And now, it seemed, they had made good on their promises, targeting him for his play.

Well, Lottie's play. His play. Whichever.

"They're trying to intimidate me over something in my play," Thatcher confessed. "But I won't be cowed by their threats. I'll stand firm and fight back."

Simms nodded in agreement. "We'll all need to tread carefully, sir. The Revivalists are not to be underestimated."

CHAPTER FOURTEEN

T HE MORNING SUN rose warm and bright over Rhodes Theatre as Lottie entered the bustling building. Her steps echoed on the polished wooden floors as she made her way toward the office they had been using to collaborate on the play. She expected to find Thatcher there, ready to work. After all, they had made significant progress with the play, and there was much to be done. "Goodrich!" she called out. "It's time to work."

To her dismay, the room was empty. The script sat abandoned on the cluttered table, untouched since their heated argument the previous day. Lottie felt her frustration simmering beneath the surface. This wasn't the time for Thatcher's flakiness.

She stormed out of the room, her long skirts swishing angrily. Lottie rarely lost her temper, but this time, her anger was justified. She had put her heart and soul into this project, and Thatcher's unexplained absence felt like a betrayal.

In the corridor outside the rehearsal room, she ran into some of the actors who were preparing for their upcoming scenes. Their faces lit up as they saw her. "Lady Lottie," one of the actors, a strapping young man named Robert, greeted her. "We were hoping you could help us with the next scene. Mr. Goodrich isn't here yet."

Lottie clenched her jaw, her vexation mounting. "Of course I'll help," she replied curtly. "But Mr. Goodrich's absence is inexcusable. I can't believe he would let down the entire production like this."

The actors nodded in agreement, sharing Lottie's disappointment. She took charge, directing them through the scene with precision and expertise. But even as she worked with the actors, her mind was racing. She couldn't shake the feeling that something was amiss with Thatcher. Where *was* he?

After the impromptu rehearsal, Lottie made her way to Rainville's office. She wasn't one to mince words, and she intended to get answers.

The duke, seated behind his cluttered desk, looked up in surprise as Lottie entered without knocking. She didn't bother with pleasantries. "Where is he?" she demanded.

Ever the picture of calm and composure, Rainville raised an eyebrow. "I beg your pardon. To whom are you referring?"

Lottie folded her arms across her chest. "Thatcher Goodrich. I need his home address."

Rainville leaned back in his chair, studying her with a thoughtful expression. "Are you certain this is the path you wish to take?"

Lottie's jaw clenched as her frustration bubbled to the surface. "I don't have time for his games! The play is on the line, and I won't let Thatcher's irresponsibility ruin it."

Relenting, the duke sighed, reaching for a piece of parchment and a quill. He scribbled down an address and handed it to Lottie. "Very well. But I would advise you to approach this matter with caution. You may find more than you bargained for."

Lottie snatched the parchment from his hand and nodded curtly. Without another word, she left his office and set out to track down Thatcher, determined to get to the bottom of his mysterious absence.

She couldn't believe Thatcher's lack of professionalism and ethics. "He simply cannot do this," she sputtered, waving her arms in exasperation. "We have a play to write, a king to please, and he's off gallivanting somewhere, probably in some tavern!"

The actors, who had gathered again to further rehearse their scenes, exchanged wary glances. Robert cleared his throat and stepped forward, attempting to calm the irate playwright. "Lady Lottie," he began, "we understand your frustration. But perhaps Mr. Goodrich has a valid reason for his absence."

Lottie turned to him with a scowl. "A valid reason? What could possibly be valid at this late a date? Robert, we are in the midst of a critical collaboration! If Mr. Goodrich has a valid reason, he should have communicated it to us. But instead, he leaves us in the lurch, doesn't he?"

Another actor, James, chimed in. "We share your concern, we do. We are just as committed to the success of this play as you are. Mr. Goodrich's absence affects us all. But I confess that I've never seen him disrespect the theatre."

Lottie let out an exasperated huff and thrust her hands on her hips. "Well, what are we supposed to do now? Sit around and wait for him to grace us with his presence?"

Robert shared a glance with James, and they exchanged a knowing nod. Then Robert stepped closer to Lottie, his voice gentle. "Lady Lottie," he said, "we can start working on the scenes that don't require Mr. Goodrich's input. We're a team, and we'll do our best to make progress without him."

James added, "And when he does return, we'll have something to show him. Perhaps this will serve as a reminder of the importance of his role in this collaboration."

Lottie eyed the actors, her initial fury beginning to ebb. She appreciated their sincerity and willingness to go on. They weren't just performers; they were her team, and they were as invested in the success of the play as she was.

With a reluctant nod, she conceded, "You're right. Let's not waste any more time. We'll work on what we can without him. But I won't let Mr. Goodrich off the hook so easily when he returns."

The actors grinned triumphantly, clearly relieved that they had successfully defused Lottie's initial outburst.

"I'll leave you to carry on," she said, and bade them farewell, eager to track the infuriating playwright down.

She embarked on a journey through the bustling streets of London, her resolve unshaken despite her frustration with Thatcher's absence.

As she made her way to his address, she couldn't help but engage in lively exchanges with the people she encountered. First, she approached a flower vendor, a plump and rosy-cheeked woman who was carefully arranging her vibrant blooms. Lottie couldn't resist stopping to admire the colorful array. "These are exquisite," she exclaimed.

The vendor beamed at the compliment. "Aren't they, miss? Fresh from the countryside this morning, they are. Would you like to purchase a bouquet?"

Lottie shook her head with a polite smile. "Not today, I'm afraid, but I appreciate the beauty you've brought to our city."

Continuing her journey, she found herself near a group of children playing a spirited game of marbles on the cobblestone street. Their laughter filled the air as they cheered each other on. "Looks like you're having a grand time," she remarked, crouching down to watch their game.

One of the children, a freckled-faced boy with tousled hair, grinned up at her. "Aye, miss! It's the best game in all of London!"

Lottie chuckled, sharing in their youthful enthusiasm for simple pleasures. "Well, carry on, then. Enjoy every moment of it." Life went by too quickly.

As she ventured farther into the heart of the city, Lottie encountered a street musician playing a melancholic tune on a violin. The haunting melody tugged at her heartstrings, and she couldn't help but pause to listen. "That's a beautiful piece," she commented, once the musician had finished.

The violinist, a kindly-looking man with a round face, nodded appreciatively. "Thank you, miss. It's a tune from my homeland, and it brings me solace." Lottie offered him a small donation as a token of her appreciation, and the musician's eyes brightened with gratitude. "May your day be filled with joy, miss," he said, his voice filled with sincerity.

With a nod and a smile, Lottie resumed her walk through the streets of London. Her impatience to confront Thatcher battled with her innate courtesy as she interacted with the people she encountered on her journey. Her determination to give him a piece of her mind remained unwavering, but she couldn't deny the instinctual politeness that guided her interactions.

As she approached a street vendor selling roasted chestnuts, the warm aroma wafted through the air, tempting her senses. She couldn't resist purchasing a small bag, even though her mind was preoccupied with thoughts of her missing collaborator.

"Ah, the chestnuts are perfect today," the vendor remarked, handing her the bag.

Lottie nodded in agreement, managing a polite smile. "Indeed, they are. Thank you."

A group of young women dressed in the latest fashion strolled by, chatting animatedly about their social plans for the evening. Lottie couldn't help but overhear their conversation and momentarily forget her frustration.

"It's Lady Clarissa's soirée tonight," one of the women exclaimed, her voice tinged with excitement.

Lottie approached them, curiosity getting the better of her. "Lady Clarissa's soirée, you say? Is it a grand affair?"

The women turned to her, their curiosity piqued by the newcomer. "Oh, yes! The finest in all of London. We've been anticipating it for weeks."

Lottie engaged in a lively conversation with the group, learning about the upcoming social event and sharing in their enthusiasm. It was another refreshing diversion from her original mission.

As she said her goodbyes and continued on her way, Lottie couldn't help but think of the many faces of London, each person with their own story and joys to share. But her resolve to confront Thatcher remained undiminished, and she pressed forward, eager to address his neglect of their work.

Finally, she made it to her destination, a small, nondescript townhouse in a once-genteel neighborhood. With shaking hands, she raised her fist and knocked.

"Good day," a gray-haired servant greeted her as the door swung open. "May I help you?"

"I'm here for Mr. Goodrich." Oh, the anger flooded back to her. "I demand to see him at once."

"He's, well, indisposed, at the moment, my lady." The tint of embarrassment in his tone told Lottie exactly how the no-good playwright was *indisposed*. "Perhaps you should come back at a later time."

Thatcher's absence this morning rushed to her mind, and her anger sparked hot. Forgetting herself, she stepped over the threshold and marched down the hall toward the stairs. "I know you're in here, Goodrich!" she shouted as she marched up them.

"My lady, I implore you," the servant begged as he rushed up the stairs and stepped around her, blocking entry to the third door on the left.

"Implore away, but I've got things to say to this man."

Lottie couldn't hide her shock as she pushed past the servant and entered Thatcher's private chamber. The sight that met her eyes left her flummoxed and speechless. There, in his bedchamber, Thatcher sat in a steaming bath, his magnificent body marred with bruises and cuts.

"Good Lord, Thatcher, what on earth happened to you?" she blurted out.

Thatcher's eyes shot open, and he winced as he moved in the bath. He seemed surprised, but his expression quickly turned guarded. "Lottie? What are you doing here?"

Ignoring his question, she rushed to his side, her fingers trembling as she reached out to touch one of the bruises on his arm. "These injuries... Did you get into a fight?"

He winced again as she touched the bruise, but he didn't pull away. "It's nothing," he muttered, clearly uncomfortable with her close scrutiny.

"Nothing?" Lottie repeated incredulously. "You look like you've been through a war. You can't just dismiss this as *nothing*."

Thatcher sighed, his shoulders slumping. "It's a long story. One I'd rather not get into right now."

Her concern deepened, and she regarded him sympathetically, but still willfully. "Well, that's just tough, because I'm not leaving until you tell me what happened. We were supposed to be working on the play together, and instead, I find you in this state."

He met her gaze, his smoky eyes filled with a complex mix of emotions. "It's complicated, Lottie. I'm afraid it involves some unsavory characters and some unfinished business."

Lottie's curiosity got the better of her, and she couldn't stop from pressing further. "Unsavory characters? Unfinished business? Thatcher, you can't keep secrets from me if they affect our work."

Thatcher sighed again, more heavily this time. "You're right, of course. But it's a long story, and I'd rather not relive it right now. Can we please discuss it later? After I've had a chance to recover?"

Lottie reluctantly nodded. "Very well, we'll discuss it later. But don't think you're off the hook. I won't let you hide this from me."

Thatcher managed a faint smile, and for a moment, the vulnerability in his eyes surprised her. "Thank you. You're...quite something."

She smiled back in exasperated affection. "Yes, well, that's why I'm here. To keep you in line and make sure you don't mess up our play."

Chapter Fifteen

L OTTIE FUSSED OVER Thatcher as he lay there in the bath, his body battered and bruised. Mindless to propriety or the fact that she was alone in a private bedchamber with a naked man—good Lord, what would her mother think?—she administered to his wounds, heat beginning a slow unfurling in the pit of her stomach at the nearness of him. At the *nakedness* of him. All those long, sculpted muscles, those broad shoulders, the dark patch of hair on his chest that led down below the water line in the most fascinating trail... Lottie's cheeks flamed, and she yanked her eyes from the water's surface just before her gaze dropped further. Avoiding eye contact, she soaked a cloth in the warm water and gently began to dab at the cuts and bruises on his face.

"Does this hurt?" she asked softly.

Thatcher winced as she touched a particularly tender spot, but gave a weak smile. "Only when you touch it."

Lottie rolled her eyes playfully. "Well, I'm trying to help you, you know."

He chuckled softly, and the tension in the room seemed to ease a bit, slowing, turning liquid and languid in a way unfamiliar to her, but that drew her like honey drew bees. "I appreciate it. I really do. It's been a very long time since anyone has tended to my care."

As she continued to tend to his injuries, she felt a growing closeness between them. Like this unexpected turn of events was bringing them together in a way that their work on the play hadn't quite managed to do. For one, the play had never landed her in his private chambers in his home.

"You should be more careful," she chided gently, sneaking a flashing glance at the dark thatch of hair teasingly just below the water's steam-fogged surface. *Drat.* It was a fascinating patch, really. One she increasingly wished to see plainly. "Getting into fights and ending up like this... It's not the behavior of a responsible playwright."

Thatcher sighed, his gaze distant. "I know it's not. But sometimes, life doesn't go as planned. There are things you can't control. Such as an attack on one's person while strolling home."

Lottie paused in her ministrations. "Good God, is *that* what happened? How dare someone accost you!" Protective anger washed through her, sending her decorum out the window. "Tell me who it is, and I'll shoot the bloody bastards." She looked him square in the eye. "I know how, you know."

He looked at her then, his eyes searching hers for something she couldn't quite identify. Emotions flashed across his sea-storm gaze, everything from amusement at her outrage, to vulnerability and shyness, before he settled into a lazy, hooded expression that turned her knees to melted butter. "Thank you. That means more to me than you know," he murmured.

In that instant, it felt as if the world around them faded away. It was just the two of them, connected by something deeper than words could convey.

"I'm here anytime you need a foul fiend dispatched with accordingly," she jested, trying to ease this rising restlessness in her body. She shifted, and her inner thighs brushed against each other under her skirts, the delicate skin lighting with sensation. Like a blush, heat bloomed between her legs, sweeping over flesh, trailing fire in its wake.

Unable to resist, she dropped her gaze once more to the water's steamy surface. "I, um," she started, quickly losing her thoughts when he shifted and water sloshed against the hard, flat plane of his belly. Her breath caught in anticipation. As the water receded, sloshing back the other way, the level lowered and she caught a glimpse of a thick, impressive manhood jutting straight as an arrow from a thatch of inky curls. "Oh my," she whispered.

It was…it was…just so *big*.

The heat between her legs flashed, went achy. Suddenly she felt plump and slick with a need she couldn't quite name. But she knew it absolutely had something to do with his thick, erect shaft, and that lazy, unreadable gaze he had locked on her.

"See something you like?" The way he said it, so soft and suggestive, sent that heat between her legs flaring a few degrees.

"I…" She trailed off, her gaze greedy on him. How could she possibly feel so shy and yet so tempted to touch? Lottie licked her lips. "I, um… That is…" Oh heavens, she couldn't contain her curiosity anymore. "*Yes*," she breathed.

She saw a whole lot of something she liked.

Every naked inch of Thatcher Goodrich.

"I was hoping you'd say that." Instantly, his large, hard hands were on her, pulling her close. One hand threaded through the hair at the back of her neck; the other boldly skimmed up her ribcage to the underside of her breast. "Christ, you're shapely," he growled, sounding hungry and pleased.

"I've never been the petite type," she murmured, her thoughts flittering away as his hot hands commanded her attention.

"Good," he said, adjusting his hand under her breast as if he was feeling its weight. "Curves are good. *Yours*." And then his mouth was on hers, hard and demanding. He pulled away long enough to order her, "Don't ever lose them."

Lottie couldn't even if she tried. It was like asking the sky not to be blue. Her shapely form just *was*. "They're acceptable?" she couldn't help asking. Much of her life she'd worried she was too statuesque, too solid, too fleshy. Just too much body, period.

Thatcher gave a harsh laugh. "Acceptable?" His stormy eyes flashed lightning hot. "What does this tell you?" With that, he lowered his hand from her breast and guided her own hand down below the waterline. "This is what your body does to me, Lottie." He placed her palm on his shaft, impossibly rigid and enlarged as it thrust toward her. "Fuck, that feels good." He groaned and watched her through hooded eyes. "You've a body made for pleasure."

"Pleasure?" she repeated, warmth spreading throughout her limbs. Oh God, his erection felt wonderful. So smooth and silky and hot, even in the water. She closed her hand into a gentle fist around him. When he groaned again and arched into her, pleasure flushed through her. How could touching him make her feel so much?

"Yes," he replied in a low tone. "Pleasure." And he closed his eyes and arched into her hand once more.

"Yours or mine?" she asked, emboldened by his response.

"Both," he whispered hotly, flexing his hips under her exploration. "When done right, the pleasure belongs to both."

"You've…experienced a lot of…pleasure…before?" How could she be envious of faceless, nameless women who'd received pleasure at the hands of this man? She knew them not. But the thought of any woman touching him where she did sent possessive want barreling straight through her. *Mine,* her everything screamed. This moody, infuriating writer was *hers.*

His hands, they were meant to explore her. Caress her. Learn her.

"There's pleasure," Thatcher said, low and seductive. "And then there's *pleasure*." As if to emphasize his point, he flexed into her, groaning softly. "You, Lottie, are pleasure with a capital P."

Well, wasn't that just the thing?

Oh, she liked that. She liked that a lot.

⋙⋘

IF LOTTIE STROKED him one more time with that sweet, innocently exploring hand of hers, he would come. Not that coming for her would be a bad thing. Her hot little hand was welcome to stroke him off anytime. Just not *this* time. "Lottie," he grunted, and dropped his head to the back of the bathtub, forgetting every single punch and bruise and cut with each delicious slide of her hand over him. "If you keep that up, this will be over before it really begins."

"You mean there's more?" Her beautiful blue eyes widened.

"There's more," he agreed, thinking of all the ways he'd like to take Lottie Castlebury. All the ways he'd like to taste her. A shiver rippled down his spine as he thought about her perfect pink womanhood and what it would taste like there, right at her slick, plump entrance. "I could show you." Please, *let me show you.* His cock throbbed with the need.

"Show me," she whispered, leaning close to capture his lips in a kiss.

It was everything Thatcher never knew he needed. Those words on her lips unlocked something long buried inside him. "Fuck yes," he growled darkly, the hedonist in him escaping. In an instant he was on his feet, water cascading off his bare skin, as he scooped Lottie into his arms and carried her to his bed. "I hope you rested well last night, love."

"Why's that?" she asked in that husky, melodic voice of hers that drove him mad with want.

Thatcher laid her on the bed, following with his big, bare body. "Because," he said, nipping her full bottom lip and settling between her lush thighs, "I'm going to keep you up all night."

"You are?"

"Mmm hmm." He nuzzled the point below her ear, inhaling her scent. "*All* night."

Lottie raised her long, curvy legs, wrapped them around his waist, and pulled him to her. He groaned at the press of his cock into her. "Showing me pleasure?"

Hunger ripped through him, and Thatcher lost it, grabbing a fistful of her skirt and yanking. The fabric ripped up the seam, exposing her to his greedy gaze. "So much fucking pleasure, my lady. Neither of us will walk for a week."

She slid a hand up his back, purring happily at the corded muscles she found there. "That sounds ominous."

"Oh, it is," he promised, need clawing at him. "Consider yourself warned."

"So warned." Her voice went even huskier, sultrier.

Thatcher gave in to his need to claim her, to touch and explore every inch of her luscious body. In moments her clothes were gone, flying across the chamber to land with a soft thump on the floorboards. "You're mine." The smile he gave her felt wolfish and wild—like his need for her.

"Show me," she whispered again, meeting his gaze with boldness and passion.

And he did. For hours, Thatcher explored her, learned her every dip, every swell, every inch of her velvet softness. Over the brink he drove her again and again, until she was limp and satiated and sighing happy little mews. Only then did he allow his own blinding climax.

Finally, in the early hours before dawn, he wrapped her against his chest, content and at peace for the first time in his life. As she drifted into blissful sleep, Thatcher stared at the ceiling, his own heart in turmoil.

Tonight changed everything.

Tonight, Thatcher fell in love.

"Bloody hell," he breathed, pulling Lottie closer. *Bloody inconvenient hell.*

What did he know about love?

Not a damn thing.

CHAPTER SIXTEEN

T HE SMALL, CANDLELIT room was filled with the rustling of papers and the soft scratching of quills as Lottie and Thatcher sat hunched over the cluttered desk. Their collaboration on the play had taken an unexpected turn as they found themselves in a constant dance of stolen glances and heart-pounding kisses, making it increasingly difficult to concentrate on their work.

Lottie's heart raced as she felt Thatcher's gaze on her, his gray eyes filled with a playful spark. "Thatcher, please," she said. "We can't afford to keep getting distracted like this. We have a play to finish."

He leaned closer, a mischievous smile playing on his lips. "But I can't seem to help myself," he replied, his voice low and husky. "You're far too captivating to resist."

She sighed, torn between the exhilaration of their mutual attraction and the frustration of their lack of progress. "This is important," she insisted. "We've been given an incredible opportunity, and we can't squander it."

He reached out, gently tracing a path along her cheek. "I know it's important," he said softly. "Yet I can't deny what I feel when I'm with you. It's like a fire burning inside me."

Lottie's cheeks flushed. "We have to keep our focus," she implored, her voice wavering. "We can't afford to let our feelings get in the way."

He nodded, his playful demeanor giving way to a more serious expression. "You're right," he admitted. "We'll find a way to balance our work and our...attraction."

Taking a deep breath, she tried to regain her composure. "Thank you," she said, her voice steadier. "Now, let's get back to the play."

She returned to the script, determined to push aside their growing feelings and focus on the task at hand. But the tension between them lingered in the air, unspoken desires that simmered beneath the surface.

She leaned in and placed a gentle peck on Thatcher's cheek, a simple gesture of affection meant to reassure him. But as her lips met his skin, something shifted between them. The kiss that had begun so innocently deepened into something more profound and tender. Their lips met in a soft, lingering kiss that spoke of unspoken emotions and a connection that went beyond mere attraction. It was a kiss that held a promise, a promise of something deeper and more meaningful than either of them had expected.

As she pulled away, their eyes met, and she saw the reflection of her own desires flickering there. It was a silent acknowledgment of the feelings growing between them, feelings that neither of them had been prepared for.

Lottie found herself at a loss for words, her emotions swirling in a dizzying whirlwind. She had always prided herself on her ability to control her own destiny, but now, in the face of this unexpected connection with Thatcher, she felt a sense of vulnerability she had never known.

Thatcher's expression mirrored her own, a mixture of longing and uncertainty. He reached out, gently cupping her cheek with his hand, his touch tender and reassuring. "Lottie," he whispered, his voice barely above a breath. "What are we doing?"

She swallowed hard, her voice trembling as she replied, "I don't know. But I do know that I can't ignore what I feel when I'm with you."

⇶⫷

"Mr. Goodrich, Lady Lottie!"

Lottie rushed out to the main stage with Thatcher, and discovered Rainville engaged in an animated discussion with a distinguished-looking nobleman. The gentleman's eyes sparkled with admiration as he gestured emphatically while speaking to the duke.

Rainville noticed Lottie and Thatcher approaching and greeted them with a warm smile. "Ah, here he is, the talented playwright!" he exclaimed. "Allow me to present Mr. Thatcher Goodrich and his assistant, Lady Lottie."

Lord Riley's eyes lit up, and he extended his hand toward Thatcher with great enthusiasm. "Mr. Goodrich, I must say, your last play was an absolute masterpiece! I was completely captivated by the storyline, the characters, the wit, and the emotion. It's a work of genius!"

Thatcher, obviously taken aback by the lavish praise, shook Lord Riley's hand with a humble nod. "Thank you, my lord," he replied, looking for all the world as if he was trying to maintain his composure. "I'm honored by your kind words."

Lottie watched the exchange, her heart sinking. Here was the very man who had taken credit for her play, basking in the praise that rightfully belonged to her. She felt the bitterness bubbling within her. How could she have forgotten even for a single moment?

Her play was an absolute masterpiece.

Her play was a work of genius.

Lord Riley turned his attention to Lottie, his gaze appraising. "And Lady Lottie, I'm certain your...contributions...whatever they may be...are notable. You clearly inspire this brilliant man to spout words that are like poetry, and I can only imagine you are quite the muse."

Lottie forced a smile, gratitude masking a layer of livid, indignant fury. "Thank you, my lord," she ground out, managing to sound polite but distant. What exactly was the lord insinuating?

As Lord Riley continued to sing praises to Thatcher, Rainville excused himself to attend to other matters. After what felt like an eternity of over-effusive compliments and congratulations, the viscount finally prepared to take his leave, promising to attend the upcoming performance of the next play.

Lottie seethed with anger as the nobleman finally departed, leaving her alone with Thatcher amidst the ornate walls of the theatre. She couldn't contain the storm of emotions churning within her. "Thatcher Goodrich, I can't believe you did it again," she spat. "You took all the credit for my work, without even blinking an eye!"

Thatcher's expression wavered between guilt and frustration. He had betrayed her trust once more, and she hoped it weighed heavily on his conscience. "Lottie, I—"

But she wasn't finished. "Do you have any idea how hard I've worked on this play? How much it means to me?" Her voice cracked, and she took a deep breath to steady herself. "And you just stood there, letting him heap praises on you, as if I didn't even exist."

⇒⟫⟩✳⟨⟪⇐

THATCHER'S SHOULDERS SLUMPED under the weight of her accusation. He knew he had wronged her, but he wasn't sure how to make amends. "I never meant for things to turn out this way," he admitted. "I... I didn't know how to tell him the truth."

Lottie's anger intensified, and her voice grew colder. "The truth? You mean the truth about how you took my work and claimed it as your own?"

Thatcher winced at her words, the pain in her eyes cutting through him like a knife. He stepped closer to her, reaching out to touch her arm, but she pulled away, unwilling to let him off the hook so easily. "Lottie, please, I understand that you're angry," he implored. "But I promise you, I will find a way to make things right. I won't let your talent go unrecognized any longer. I swear."

She shook her head, her disappointment palpable. "It's not just about recognition," she said. "It's about trust, about honesty. You've betrayed both." As the weight of her words settled between them, she turned and began to walk away, adding, "I can't bear to stay in your presence any longer, not when my heart aches with the knowledge that the man I was growing to care for has let me down in such a profound way."

Thatcher watched her retreating figure, his heart heavy with regret. He knew that mending their fractured relationship would be an uphill battle. One of enormous proportions. But he would prove to Lottie that he was worth forgiving, even if it meant revealing the truth about the play to the whole world and risking everything he had worked so hard to achieve.

CHAPTER SEVENTEEN

T HE GAS LAMPS created a hazy atmosphere that reflected Thatcher's conflicted state of mind. He walked with a heavy gait, his boots scuffing against the uneven stones. The city, which had once been his muse and his escape, now felt oppressive. As he continued his solitary journey, he revisited the argument with Lottie they'd had at Rhodes Theatre. Her words echoed in his mind, each one a painful reminder of his deception. It was a bitter irony that he, a playwright known for his sharp wit and clever dialogue, found himself speechless in her presence, unable to explain or justify his actions.

"Stealing her work," he muttered. "What a fool I am."

The night air was cool against his skin, but it did little to ease the chaos within him. He was a man torn between desire and guilt, his heart and conscience waging an awful, relentless battle. Thatcher had always prided himself on his quick thinking and cunning, but when it came to Lottie, he had been blindsided by emotions he couldn't quite comprehend. Never had he met a woman like her. Lottie possessed a rare combination of intelligence, passion, and a fierce determination to prove herself in a world that most often dismissed women's abilities. Her talent was undeniable. Yet, in a moment of weakness and arrogance, he had robbed her of the recognition she deserved.

His footsteps echoed in the empty streets, each hollow sound a reminder of his recklessness. Their heated argument replayed in his mind. The fire in her eyes, the intensity of her words—they had seared themselves into his memory. Into his *heart*.

"What was I thinking?" he muttered. "To take her work and claim it as my own..." But his remorse went beyond even that. It was the way she had looked at him, not just with anger but with a deep disappointment. Christ, it had pierced his heart. In that moment, he had seen something more than just frustration in her gaze. He had seen *hurt*.

As he reached a quieter, barely lit corner of the street, he slowed to a stop. He leaned against a lamppost, his frustration and self-loathing threatening to consume him. "She deserves better," he muttered to himself, closing his eyes briefly as he felt the weight of his actions. "And I should *be* better."

As he resumed his walk, a sense of desolation settled over him. It was a feeling he had grown accustomed to over the years, born out of his shite childhood and the struggles that had defined his early years as a writer. He had fought tooth and nail to claw his way to success, and yet here he was, making the same mistakes he had once sworn to avoid. He remembered the countless nights he had spent alone, hunched over his desk in his small, shabby townhouse, penning plays that had captured the hearts of Londoners. He had grown up with a drunk for a father, the youngest son in a family struggling to maintain their faded wealth. Hopeless and tired, his mother had fled his father's ale-fueled fists, leaving him to awaken to his tenth birthday motherless.

It had been a harsh upbringing, one that had taught him the value of cunning and wit. He had learned to use his words as weapons, earning money through his razor-sharp tongue and insight into the human condition. For years, he had lived like a poor artist, scraping by and relying on his words to survive. But he had persevered, and eventually, he had achieved the success he had so desperately craved. He had become a celebrated playwright, his name known and respected throughout London. Yet, even with his accomplishments, he couldn't escape the chip on his shoulder, the lingering resentment of the hardships he had endured.

Why wasn't it enough?

Thatcher's walking path led him through the winding streets of Covent Garden, where he sought refuge at the Meadowlark Tavern. It was a place where he could drown his sorrows in drink and escape the demands of his own conscience.

West greeted him with a nod. Thatcher took a seat at the bar, his thoughts still heavy with guilt and frustration. He signaled for a drink, and West poured a glass of whiskey without a word.

As Thatcher took a sip of the fiery liquid, he wondered if he was destined to repeat the mistakes of his past. He had worked so hard to escape the shadows of his upbringing, to become a man of substance and success. And yet here he was, haunted by his own actions and the consequences they might bring. He was staring into the depths of his glass, lost in thought, when West finally broke the silence.

The bartender's voice was low and measured as he began to speak, his words carrying the weight of advice long held in silence. "We all carry our burdens, Thatcher. It's how we choose to bear them that defines us."

Thatcher's gaze shot to West, shock rippling through him. *How does he know?* His thoughts were a whirlwind of emotions as he finished his drink and prepared to leave the tavern. Thatcher knew he had a choice to make, a chance to make amends for his actions. But it wouldn't be easy. With women, it never was.

With one last nod to West, Thatcher stepped back out into the cool, unforgiving night. A man at a crossroads, he gave a mighty, forceful sigh. Damn facing the consequences of his actions and the chance for redemption in the eyes of the woman who had captured his heart. Self-reflection hurt.

Suddenly, chaos erupted in the streets. Thatcher's senses sharpened as he heard the round of shouts and the clatter of hooves against cobblestones. He turned to see a carriage hurtling toward him, its wheels spinning wildly as it careened around a corner, its driver struggling to regain control.

"Move!" someone shouted, the urgency in their voice sending a jolt of fear through him.

His instincts kicked in, and he tried to leap to the side, but it was too late. The carriage bore down on him with terrifying speed. Before he could react, it struck him with a bone-jarring impact.

Everything went black.

>>>><<<<

THATCHER'S EYES SHOT open, and he immediately knew something was terribly wrong. The tight confines of the carriage pressed in around him, and the air inside was stifling. Panic clawed at his chest as he realized he was alone in the darkness. Frantically, he fumbled for the latch on the carriage door, but his hands found nothing but smooth wood. He pushed against the door with all his might, but it remained stubbornly shut.

A rush of fear surged through him as he considered the possibilities. How had he ended up here? The last thing he remembered was being struck by the runaway carriage, and then he'd blacked out.

The answer came to him in a chilling realization. The crest on the carriage door—the emblem of a nobleman he knew. Edward Waverly. He'd been inside, dressed all in black, a face mask rolled up, grinning wildly. Ah, bloody hell, he was part of the Revivalists! Thatcher had heard whispers about their crimes, read the news sheets, knew they dressed all in black. Dread coursed through him as he realized the implications.

What did Edward want with him? They were friends! Damn it, *damn it!*

He contemplated his predicament. The Revivalists were known for their secrecy and ruthlessness. If they had abducted him, it could only mean trouble. Desperation motivated him as he renewed his efforts to escape the carriage. He kicked at the door, heaved his shoulder against it, and yelled for help, though he knew the chances of anyone hearing him were slim.

Time seemed to stretch on endlessly as he struggled, the darkness pressing in around him. Fear and uncertainty gnawed at his mind, and he couldn't help but wonder what fate awaited him at the hands of the Revivalists. The air inside the carriage grew increasingly oppressive, and he felt sweat bead on his forehead, his shirt clinging uncomfortably to his skin. The faint light filtering through the gaps in the door revealed the small space, adorned with plush, worn upholstery and intricate carvings on the wooden panels.

Outside, he could hear the muffled sounds of the bustling city—the clip-clop of horses' hooves on cobblestones, the distant calls of street vendors, and the indistinct voices of passersby. But inside this confined prison, he was isolated, trapped in a world of shadows and uncertainty.

His mind raced with questions. About Edward. About the Revivalists. Why had they targeted him? What did they want? And perhaps most pressing of all, was there any hope of his escape? He continued to struggle against the door, and his fingers found a small latch nestled discreetly near the handle. With a surge of hope, he grasped it and pushed, praying that it might release him from this hell.

The latch gave way with a soft click, and the door swung open slightly. A rush of cool, fresh air filled the carriage, carrying with it the distant scents of the city—a mix of horse manure, freshly baked bread, and the faint aroma of blooming flowers. Thatcher's heart pounded with fear and rising fury. With one final, desperate push, he flung the door wide open and tumbled out onto the cobbled street. His body ached from the fall, but the pain was nothing compared to the relief he felt at being free.

He looked around, trying to get his bearings. The street was unfamiliar to him, a narrow alleyway flanked by tall, imposing buildings that loomed overhead. It was a quiet corner of the city, tucked away from the main thoroughfares, and he could hear the distant sounds of church bells tolling the hour. Thatcher knew he had to be cautious. If the Revivalists were still nearby, they might be watching for any sign of his escape. He picked himself up. The world around him was a blur of gaslit lanterns, flickering shadows, and the occasional glimpse of a passerby. Every sound, every movement, sent a jolt of anxiety through him. He couldn't afford to let his guard down.

"Ahoy! What do you think you're doing?" a hard voice demanded from behind.

Thatcher's heart skipped several beats as he heard the harsh, aristocratic voice. Panic surged through him, and he froze, his hand still gripping the broken latch of the carriage door. Slowly, he turned to face the source of the voice, and his eyes met those of a tall, imposing figure who had materialized at the side of the carriage. The man was impeccably dressed in a dark, tailored coat and a finely knotted cravat, his face partially obscured by the shadows cast by the gaslit lanterns.

Edward Waverly.

With a sinking, sick feeling, Thatcher realized that his friend was indeed a member of the Revivalists, the group responsible for terrorizing London and killing innocent men and women. *Blast it!* He had hoped to slip away unnoticed, to escape the clutches of his captors, but it seemed that his plan had been foiled.

"I believe I've taken a wrong turn," Thatcher bluffed anyway, trying to keep his voice steady despite the rising fear within him. He forced himself to meet the man's gaze directly. "I'll just be on my way."

Edward regarded him with a cold, calculating expression, his lips curving into a humorless smile. He barely resembled the amiable thespian Thatcher knew. "Leaving so soon, Mr. Goodrich?" he asked, his tone laced with a chilling edge. "You've been quite the elusive quarry. We've been waiting for this opportunity."

"Who's we?" Thatcher dared to ask. His mind raced as he

assessed his options. He couldn't afford to be captured again, not when he had just managed to escape. He knew that he had to act quickly and decisively. He'd ask the question of why Edward later. Much later. Once he was safe and still alive.

With a sudden burst of energy, Thatcher lunged at Edward, catching him off guard. They grappled in the dimly lit alley, their breath coming in harsh gasps as they struggled for control. The sounds of their scuffle echoed off the narrow walls, and for a moment, it seemed as though the outcome hung in the balance. Though lean, Edward was surprisingly tough and strong.

Thatcher fought with all the desperation of a man determined to regain his safety. He knew that his life depended on it, and he couldn't afford to lose this battle. But Edward was strong and relentless, and the odds were stacked against Thatcher. As they grappled, he plotted. He needed a way out, a means of escape that would allow him to slip through Edward's grasp and disappear into the dark, snaking streets of London once more. His heart roared in his chest as he searched for an opening, a moment of weakness that he could exploit.

The outcome remained uncertain, but Thatcher knew that he couldn't afford to back down.

As the struggle continued with grunts and thuds echoing in the dark alley, a blinding light suddenly pierced through the gloom. Thatcher's eyes, adjusted to the dimness, were momentarily shocked, and he instinctively shielded his face from the intense illumination.

Edward, taking advantage of his momentary blindness, pushed him away and stepped back, holding a torch just lit, its harsh bright brilliance bursting upon Thatcher's disheveled form. Blinking rapidly to regain his vision, Thatcher squinted at Edward, now looming over him.

With a sinister grin, Edward spoke, his voice dripping with malice. "It's time for you to pay for all those things you wrote in your play, Thatcher. The Revivalists do not take such matters lightly, and I've been picked to dispatch of you."

Thatcher's heart sank as he realized the gravity of his situation. The Revivalists were not just thugs; they were a powerful and dangerous organization of aristocrats with a reach that extended into the highest echelons of Society. They had taken offense with something in his play, and now they sought retribution.

What had he written?

"Which play, exactly, do you all take such offense with?" He squinted against the torch flare. "I've written so many." He needed a plan, a way to outsmart his captor and slip away once more. So he stalled. "Too many to count on both hands, if you can believe that."

Edward seemed to anticipate his every move, keeping the blinding light fixed on Thatcher and maintaining a safe distance. It was clear that he had been trained for encounters like these, and Thatcher realized that he was facing a formidable adversary. Not his friend. Not an actor. A foe. An *enemy*.

Thatcher cleared his throat, trying to keep his voice steady despite the fear gnawing at him. "You've got it all wrong," he began, his words measured. "The play was just fiction, a work of art. It wasn't meant to offend anyone."

The man's laughter was cold and heartless. "Fiction, you say? Do you take us Revivalists for fools, Thatcher? The words you penned struck a chord with our organization, and we do not take such things in stride. Oh no, we react with punishing swiftness."

How to convince this zealot that he was not a threat, that his words were merely a product of his imagination? Edward's fanaticism made reason and logic unlikely to prevail.

With the light still blinding him, Thatcher weighed his options. His life hung in the balance. He had to find a way to escape the clutches of the Revivalists. His trusted friend was not his friend at all, but rather a crazed, immoral beast who wanted him dead.

Oh, and he was madly in love with the woman he'd stolen from.

God, he missed the simplicity of his writer's block.

CHAPTER EIGHTEEN

T HE NEXT DAY dawned with a sense of anticipation that fluttered in Lottie's chest like a trapped butterfly. Her heart raced as she went about her morning routine, preparing for a day that she hoped would bring long-awaited clarity and resolution. She couldn't wait any longer to confront her feelings for Thatcher, to confess what had been burgeoning within her for so long.

Her steps were light as she walked through the bustling streets of London, making her way to Rhodes Theatre. The city seemed to hum with its usual vibrancy, but her thoughts were singularly focused on the man who had occupied her mind and heart. Today was the day she would finally speak her truth, no matter the outcome. "Thatcher Goodrich, here I come."

As she reached the theatre, her spirits soared, only to plummet when she realized that Thatcher was not there. "What the devil?" She scanned the theatre, hoping to catch a glimpse of his familiar figure or hear the sound of his voice, but there was no sign of him.

Worry began to creep into her chest, squeezing her heart in an iron grip. Where could he be? Had something happened to him? Lottie's mind raced through a litany of possibilities, each more dire than the last. She knew she had to find him, to make sure he was safe and sound.

Unable to wait any longer, she rushed out of the theatre and set off toward Thatcher's townhouse, her feet carrying her with a sense of urgency that she didn't understand. Her insides screamed that something was amiss. The journey seemed endless as her mind raced ahead, contemplating the words she would say once she found Thatcher, the emotions she would reveal.

Finally, she arrived at his small townhouse. With trembling hands, she reached out and knocked on the door, hoping against hope that he would answer, that she would find him inside, safe and unharmed and happy to receive her profession of love.

But there was no answer.

The door remained stubbornly closed, and a sinking feeling settled in the pit of Lottie's stomach. She couldn't shake the worry that had gripped her since the morning. Where could Thatcher be? She considered her options. Should she wait for him to return? Should she seek out Rainville to inquire about his whereabouts? Every moment of uncertainty weighed anxiously on her, and she longed to see Thatcher's face, to look into his stormy eyes and finally tell him how she felt.

With a deep breath, she decided to wait. Perching herself on the doorstep, she gazed out at the bustling street, her mind filled with thoughts of the man she had come to care for so deeply. She hoped that he would return soon.

Time seemed to slow as Lottie sat there, the world around her carrying on at its usual pace. The sun moved lazily across the sky, casting shifting shadows on the cobblestone streets. People bustled by, their voices a distant murmur as she watched and waited, her heart heavy with concern. Each passing minute felt like an eternity, and her doubt began to gnaw at her. What if something had happened to Thatcher? What if he needed her help, and she was stuck waiting here, powerless to assist him? The weight of her worry threatened to crush her spirits, and she yearned for some sign, some indication that he was safe.

At last, after what felt like an eternity, the door to Thatcher's townhouse creaked open, and Lottie's heart leaped with hope. She turned her gaze eagerly toward the entrance, ready to see him stride out, his charismatic smile lighting up his features. But the figure that emerged was not Thatcher.

Instead, it was his servant, the older man she'd met that once, with weathered features and a stern countenance. He regarded Lottie with a mixture of curiosity and suspicion, as if wondering why she was sitting on the doorstep. "Can I help you, miss?" he inquired.

Lottie struggled to find her voice, the knot of worry still tight in her chest. "I... I'm looking for Mr. Goodrich," she managed.

The man's brow furrowed as he studied her. "Mr. Goodrich isn't here," he replied, his tone matter-of-fact.

Lottie's heart sank. "Do you know where he is?" she pressed.

The servant hesitated for a moment before responding. "He didn't tell me where he went," he admitted. "Is there something you need from him?"

Lottie hesitated. "I... I was just worried when I couldn't find him," she confessed, her voice softer now.

The servant's expression softened, and he seemed to understand the genuine concern in Lottie's eyes. "Mr. Goodrich can be a bit unpredictable," he said with a sigh. "But he's a resourceful man. I'm sure he's just got himself wrapped up in something or other."

Lottie nodded, though her worry had not entirely dissipated. "Thank you," she said.

The servant nodded in acknowledgment and then retreated back into the townhouse, leaving Lottie once again alone on the doorstep. She sighed, her heart heavy with unanswered questions and unresolved emotions. Though she had come here with the intention of confessing her feelings to Thatcher, she now found herself consumed by a different concern—his well-being. Where could he be, and what could he possibly be wrapped up in?

Determined not to let her anxiety overwhelm her, Lottie resolved to wait a little longer. She couldn't shake the feeling that she needed to be there for him, no matter the circumstances. And so, with her heart a wobbly mess, she continued her vigil on the doorstep, watching the world go by as she waited for Thatcher's return.

The servant must have noticed that she was still sitting on the doorstep, her worry etched across her face like a map of her fears. For, with a heavy sigh, he opened the door to approach her once more. He stepped out onto the doorstep, his brows knitted in a deep frown. "My lady, I hate to intrude," he began, his voice gruffer than before, "but it isn't usual for Mr. Goodrich to be away this long without a word."

Lottie turned toward the servant. "You're worried too, aren't you?" she asked, her voice soft.

The servant hesitated for a moment before nodding, his gruff exterior softening. "Aye, my lady," he admitted. "It isn't like him to disappear like this. I've known him long enough to sense when something's amiss."

Lottie nodded in understanding. She hadn't known Thatcher as long as his servant had, but even in their short time working together, she had come to realize that he was a man of routine, someone who rarely deviated from his usual patterns. This unexpected absence was cause for concern.

"I just want to make sure he's safe," Lottie said. "I don't know where he could be or what trouble he might have gotten himself into."

The servant regarded her with a new look of empathy. "I appreciate your concern," he said. "Let me see if I can find out anything more. Mr. Goodrich might not always be forthcoming, but he trusts me enough to share his whereabouts when he's ready."

Lottie nodded gratefully, her heart warmed by the man's willingness to help. She watched as he disappeared once more into the townhouse, his resolve to uncover the mystery of Thatcher's absence evident in his every step.

As she waited once more on the doorstep, Lottie couldn't help but feel a strange connection with the man inside. They shared a common concern for Thatcher—the worry for his safety. Sometimes it was nice to know one wasn't always alone.

What seemed like hours passed as she waited on that door-step for Thatcher's man to return. She plucked at loose threads on her dress as she waited. She admired the crisp and colorful autumn leaves drifting down from the tree to her left and waited. She paced and sat and paced and sat some more. She searched for shapes in the clouds that drifted by overhead. And she waited.

Waited.

Waited.

Finally, the door cracked open, and a figure stepped out.

"Let's go find our playwright, shall we?" the servant asked, setting a brisk pace.

"We shall." Lottie hopped up from the doorstep, her legs protesting the sudden movement with ill-timed cramping. "Most definitely, Mr....?"

"Simms, my lady. They call me Simms."

"Nice to meet you, Mr. Simms."

"I apologize for keeping you waiting. It took an excruciatingly long time for my missive to be returned with the information I sought."

"Not a concern at all." She waved it off. All that mattered was that they located Thatcher and that he was unharmed.

They set off, eagerness fueling her feet. But one delay after another slowed them down. First it was the fruit vendor's overturned cart blocking the way. Then it was the wagon unloading bolt after bolt of fabric in the middle of the street. And then it was the group of lads loading piles and piles of scandal rags into their cart and doing fine until a binding slipped and sheets blew all over the lane in a blinding parchment storm.

The sun hung heavy in the afternoon sky, casting a late-day glow over the winding streets of London when they finally, fully got underway. Lottie's nerves were stretched taut by that point, to say the least.

Gas lamps flickered and sputtered to life, creating pools of flickering light that danced on the cobbled pathways. Their footsteps echoed through the narrow, winding alleyways, leading them deeper into the heart of the city. London was alive with whispered secrets and the distant echoes of laughter from taverns and inns. Yet, as they ventured further from the familiar streets, the city's cacophony faded into a distant murmur.

The air grew cooler, carrying with it the scent of damp earth and the distant murmur of the Thames. Lady Lottie's heart raced with each step, growing apprehension fueling her search. She couldn't shake the sense that something was terribly amiss as their journey took them past derelict buildings and deserted factories. The city's once-thriving heart had given way to shadows and solitude. It was here that their quest led them to the looming structure of an old flour mill.

"Why are we stopping here?" Lottie whispered, afraid to speak any louder for fear the building might crumble from the sound of her voice.

"This is where Thatcher used to come to write his plays. Said he liked the quiet and the air of neglect. Said it spoke to him. For years it was his favorite place."

Lottie didn't understand and scrunched her nose in confusion. "That makes little sense to me. Why would a crumbling flour mill inspire him?"

"Because it used to belong to his father, Baron Goodrich, before he lost it and the family fortune in a drunken card game."

Oh.

"Over time it became a regular rehearsal place for Thatcher and his actors. Long before his time at Rhodes. It's been some time since he's used it, but I got my gut telling me we'll find him here. The missive I received earlier confirmed that recently lights have been spotted through the windows inside late at night."

That made as much sense as anything. "Lead on," she said, gesturing ahead of them.

The mill stood like a forgotten giant, its timeworn bricks weathered by centuries of wind and rain. It cast a forbidding silhouette against the moonlit sky. Lottie and Simms exchanged a glance, their unspoken understanding solidifying their resolve.

As they approached the mill's imposing entrance, a creaking sound echoed through the silence, like a whisper of hidden secrets. The massive doors, aged and rusted, hung partially ajar, inviting them into the darkness within. Lottie's stomach clenched as they stepped into the mill, their footsteps muffled by the layer of dust that covered the wooden floors. Shafts of moonlight filtered through cracks in the dilapidated roof, creating eerie patterns of light and shadow.

Simms, a pillar of strength and determination, led the way, his senses alert to the slightest disturbance. Lottie followed closely, her thoughts consumed by worry for Thatcher. As they ventured deeper into the mill, they came upon a chamber filled with forgotten looms, a testament to a time when this place had been alive and functioning. Cobwebs clung to the ancient contraptions, and the air was heavy with the scent of decay.

"Let's look through here." Simms gestured through the doorway ahead of him.

Their search led them further into the bowels of the mill, where they discovered a narrow staircase, its wooden steps groaning with each ascent. Lottie's pulse quickened as they climbed higher, uncertainty gnawing at her. At the top of the staircase, they found themselves in a small chamber, its walls lined with decaying sacks of flour. Thatcher sat slumped against them, battered and bruised, his eyes wide with fear.

"Thatcher!" she cried.

A man stepped before them, cloaked in shadows, his presence menacing and malevolent. He held a lantern, its feeble light casting long, eerie shadows across the room.

Thatcher's voice trembled as he spoke, his words filled with desperation and defiance. "You shouldn't have come," he whispered, his eyes darting between Lottie and Simms. "It's the Revivalists."

Simms's gaze remained fixed on the mysterious figure, his instincts clearly alert and ready for whatever might come next. And she, though frightened, stood her ground, determined to rescue the man she had come to love.

The room held its breath and waited.

CHAPTER NINETEEN

TENSION HUNG THICK in the air, ripe with the scent of confrontation, as Edward Waverly, a member of the despicable Revivalists, driven by fervent ideology, advanced upon them with dangerous intent.

Edward, his face twisted in zealous anger, brandished a crude weapon—a makeshift cudgel fashioned from a piece of discarded loom. His eyes glinted with fanatical conviction as he raged against the perceived transgressions of Thatcher's play. "You thought you could corrupt women with your blasphemous words!" he bellowed, his voice reverberating through the chamber. "To think, that you would pen such heresy and spread it like a plague!"

Thatcher, battered and bruised but appearing undaunted, countered with equal force. "I merely sought to tell a story, to explore the human condition, to provoke thought and discussion." Though he still wasn't entirely sure which play they were talking about. One of his...or Lottie's? The play everyone thought was his.

Simms suddenly moved with practiced precision, positioning himself between Lottie and the Revivalist. His eyes bored into the zealot. "I'll not let him harm you, my lady."

But Lottie, her fiery spirit unbroken even if shaken, spoke up in defiance. "Your beliefs about the natural order of the world are outdated and oppressive. Women are not inferior, and men like you will no longer dictate our lives!"

"Good God, what is this heresy?" With an enraged cry, the Revivalist lunged forward, swinging his crude weapon. A fierce struggle ensued.

Lottie's quick thinking saved them all from the brink of peril. She seized an abandoned sack of flour, sending its contents billowing into the air like a powdery veil. The chamber was thrown into disarray, visibility reduced to mere inches. Amidst the choking cloud, Thatcher and Edward stumbled and grappled with one another, their movements erratic and disoriented.

Simms, waiting until the perfect moment, then managed to disarm the Revivalist with a swift and calculated strike, rendering the man defenseless.

As the flour settled and the chamber grew calm once more, Lottie stood victorious but weary. The Revivalist, his fervor extinguished, lay defeated.

It was in the aftermath of this confrontation that they learned the true motivation behind the man's rage.

Simms got him talking.

The servant had a way.

Edward and other Revivalists had taken issue with a character in Lottie's play, one that challenged the conventional notions of male superiority and the subservience of women. The character's defiance had struck a chord with the Revivalists, prompting Edward to confront Thatcher and prevent him from further "corrupting" women's minds.

"This play you've penned, Goodrich, it's nothing but a cesspool of wickedness and defiance! You think you can just spew these vile words and turn women against their rightful place? You're mistaken if you believe I'll stand idly by!" Edward's voice shook with anger.

"I penned this play to explore the depths of human emotion and challenge the norms that bind us. It was never meant to harm anyone," Thatcher replied, his voice steady and firm.

Edward's eyes blazed with righteous indignation. "Harm?

Harm, you say? You dare to suggest that your words, your poison, aren't dangerous? Women have been obedient, virtuous, and content with their place in society for centuries, and you seek to upend it all with your devilish fantasies!"

Lottie butted in. "We women refuse to be oppressed any longer! Your beliefs about women's subservience are outdated and unjust. We demand equality and respect."

"Equality? Respect?" Edward's voice dripped with disdain. "You women should be thankful for the protection and guidance of your husbands and fathers. You'll bring ruin upon yourselves with your foolish notions of independence."

"Our world is changing, Edward, and it's time we acknowledge that," Thatcher replied, his tone growing weary. "We must move forward, embracing progress and equality for all."

Edward thrashed his head, yelling, "Progress? Equality? I'll have none of it! Men are the rightful rulers of this world, and no amount of your seditious words will change that. You'll all be held accountable for your treacherous beliefs!"

"Your narrow-mindedness blinds you to the potential of a more just and inclusive society. Women won't be silenced, and we won't back down." Lottie's voice was steel.

The exchange continued, heated and impassioned, as each side defended their beliefs with unwavering determination. The clash of ideologies echoed through the air.

Amidst the fervent argument, Thatcher believed they had quelled the Revivalist's anger, but was gravely mistaken. As the tension in the room seemed to simmer down, Edward seized a moment of opportunity. With a sudden burst of rage and a primal scream, he lunged at Lottie, his hands outstretched in a menacing grip. *"Die, bitch!"* he roared.

Simms moved with lightning speed. He snatched a pointed piece of old loom from the grimy floor and drove it into the Revivalist's ear, the long shard penetrating Edward's skull with a gruesome finality. A guttural cry escaped his lips, but it was cut short as his body went limp and crumpled to the floor.

The room fell into a chilling silence.

⟫⟫⟫⟩⟨⟪⟪⟪

LOTTIE STARED WIDE-EYED at the lifeless form of her would-be assailant, her breaths coming in ragged gasps. Her heart thundered in her chest, and she felt a strange mixture of terror and gratitude wash over her. Without Simms's intervention, her fate might have been far bleaker.

She was struck by the profound impact her words had unwittingly wrought. She had never intended to incite such a violent response; her aim had been to shed light on the struggles and aspirations of the human spirit. And yet, here they three stood, survivors of a harrowing encounter with a man whose fanaticism knew no bounds.

Thatcher, his face drained of color, approached Lottie with a mixture of concern and relief. "Are you all right?" he whispered, his voice barely audible in the eerie quiet that enveloped them.

She nodded, unable to speak, her gaze still fixed on the corpse. Simms, his hands trembling, withdrew the bloodstained piece of weaving loom, his grim expression revealing the gravity of his actions.

In that blood-smeared chamber of the old flour mill, they were confronted with the consequences and perilous depths to which some would go to defend their beliefs. Edward Waverly, whose misogynistic convictions had driven him to violence, now lay defeated, a grim testament to the power of conviction, the fragility of life, and the lengths to which one could go to protect their crazed beliefs.

"We should go now," Lottie whispered, needing very much to be elsewhere.

⟫⟫⟫⟩⟨⟪⟪⟪

THEY MADE THEIR way back to Rhodes Theatre and sent Simms to alert the authorities. Before he left, Lottie turned to him. "Thank you for saving my life."

"I don't need thanks for that." He waved her off.

Lottie nodded, understanding. "Now, listen carefully. You must go to Bow Street headquarters and find my brother, Captain Catamount Castlebury. Tell him everything that transpired tonight. Make sure you don't omit any details. Tell him where the mill is located."

Simms nodded. "Of course, Lady Lottie. I'll do as you say."

She continued, her voice firm, "You must stress that we were threatened and attacked. Tell him about the body in the flour mill and that the man who's now deceased was a Revivalist. This could be a matter of utmost importance. You must impress upon him the need for secrecy and discretion. We don't know who else might be involved."

"I'll find him, and I'll make sure he understands the gravity of the situation. You have my word."

Lottie smiled gratefully, touched by Simms's loyalty and commitment to their safety. "Thank you. Please, go quickly. We'll be waiting for your return."

With that, the servant hurried off into the night, leaving Lottie and Thatcher to grapple with the aftermath of their harrowing encounter. They made their way back to the main stage of the Theatre, leaving behind the gruesome scene in the abandoned flour mill. As they stepped through the theatre's backstage entrance, they were met with a flurry of concerned faces—actors, stagehands, and Rainville himself.

He rushed forward to meet them. "Lottie, Thatcher, where have you been? We were beginning to fear the worst."

Lottie, still shaken by the night's events, took a moment to compose herself. "It's a long story. There's a body in an abandoned flour mill on the outskirts of London."

Rainville's eyes widened in surprise, and he exchanged a quick glance with Thatcher. "A body, you say? Are you both unharmed?"

Thatcher stepped forward. "We're unharmed, but it's not a pleasant sight, I assure you."

Rainville nodded. "Revivalists?"

"Revivalists," Lottie and Thatcher agreed.

"Shite. I'll tell Catamount."

Before they could stop him to tell him that alerting her brother had already been done, Rainville hurried off down the lane.

The actors who had been waiting anxiously approached. One of the leading actors, a tall, distinguished man, spoke up, his voice filled with concern. "What happened? You both look as though you've seen a ghost."

Lottie exchanged a glance with Thatcher, silently deciding that some explanation was warranted. She took a deep breath and began to recount the harrowing events of the evening, from the Revivalist's appearance to the violent confrontation in the mill. The actors listened in stunned silence as she spoke, their expressions growing graver with each passing moment. It was a tale that defied belief.

When she finished her account, there was a heavy silence, broken only by the distant sounds of Rainville's hurried retreating footsteps.

The actor, clearly shaken, spoke up. "This is madness, absolute madness. What kind of man would go to such lengths over a *play*?"

Thatcher chimed in, "An extremist, blinded by his own beliefs. We were fortunate to escape with our lives." They had decided not to tell them *who* the madman was. They'd all find out it was Edward soon enough. The shock could be dealt with then.

The other actors nodded in agreement, their faces etched with concern. It was clear that the gravity of the situation had left a deep impression on all of them.

As they waited the authorities to arrive, Lottie found herself at the center of a tense and somber atmosphere. The events of the night had shattered the illusion of her safety, reminding her that she was not immune to the dangers that lurked in the shadows of London's streets.

>>><<<

THATCHER TOOK LOTTIE'S hand gently. "Lottie," he began, "I owe you a profound apology. That day, when I took your journal, it was a terrible violation of your trust, and I can't express how deeply sorry I am."

Lottie's gaze met his, her eyes showing a mix of surprise and uncertainty. She listened intently, appearing unsure of what to expect from his confession.

"I not only took your words," Thatcher continued, his voice trembling with remorse, "but I took your work, your brilliance, your heart and soul, and I claimed it as my own. It was a despicable act, one that I deeply regret."

He turned to the actors and a returned Rainville. "I must also confess that I've been struggling with writer's block for some time. Lottie's journal was a beacon of inspiration that I couldn't resist, and I deceived you all by presenting her work as mine."

Rainville's stern expression softened as he listened, considering Thatcher's admission. The actors exchanged glances, their expressions of surprise and sympathy.

Thatcher continued, "I know my actions have caused harm, not only to you, Lottie, but to all of you who have worked tirelessly on this play. I don't expect forgiveness, but I promise to make it right. Lottie, I will give you the credit you deserve for your incredible contribution to our play, and as the true writer of my last work."

Lottie's eyes welled up with tears as she listened to his heartfelt apology and confession. Christ, he felt vulnerable. But she needed it. Deserved it from him. She nodded, her voice choked with emotion. "Thank you. I appreciate your honesty."

Rainville stepped forward. "Thatcher, you have much to

atone for, but your willingness to set things right is a step in the right direction. We will work together to give Lady Lottie the recognition she truly deserves. But know that trust, once broken, takes time to rebuild."

Thatcher nodded. "I understand, and I'm prepared to face the consequences of my actions. From this moment on, I will be honest and transparent in all matters."

His words hung in the air, heavy with his remorse. The theatre was filled with a profound silence as he stood before the gathered company, the pale lamplight casting long shadows across his face. In that stillness, the crackling tension of the past moments began to dissipate.

With that, the tension in the theatre eased, and a collective sense of resolution filled the space. It was a turning point, a moment of redemption.

➤➤➤❮❮❮

LOTTIE'S HEART SWELLED with a mixture of emotions as she watched him. She had expected to confront him, to be met with resistance and defensiveness, but his heartfelt apology had caught her off guard. There was a vulnerability in his eyes that she hadn't seen before, and it tugged at her heart.

His voice had quivered with sincerity, every word a testament to the depth of his remorse. It was as if he was laying bare his soul for all to see, not just admitting to taking her journal but to the theft of her talent and passion, to the very essence of her creativity. She could see the weight of his actions bearing down on him, and it was clear that he genuinely regretted his choices.

The faces of the actors in the theatre were a mosaic of reactions. Surprise, empathy, and a glimmer of hope danced in their eyes. Thatcher's revelation had unveiled a man who was flawed but capable of self-reflection and change. The fragile threads of trust that had been severed were now being carefully rewoven, strand by strand.

Rainville's gaze was fixed on Thatcher as if he were seeing him in a new light. He clearly understood the significance of this moment, that it was a turning point for their collaboration and for Thatcher himself.

As Thatcher vowed to give Lottie the credit she deserved, she found herself overwhelmed with gratitude. She had spent years striving to make her voice heard, to gain recognition as a talented playwright, and now, through his apology, Thatcher had offered her the acknowledgment she had so longed for.

Her teary-eyed nod of acceptance conveyed her appreciation, and she felt a glimmer of hope that their partnership could be based on trust and genuine collaboration.

"Well then," Rainville said, "if we're to move forward and create the masterpiece we aspire to, let's do so with Lady Lottie's brilliance rightfully acknowledged."

The actors broke into spontaneous applause. They appreciated a story, and this one was better than any they had ever performed on stage.

Thatcher, though visibly relieved, held his gaze on Lottie. The mixture of vulnerability, sincerity, and determination in his eyes spoke volumes, as he confessed to taking her journal.

Lottie, now more certain than ever about her own emotions, met his gaze with a soft, knowing smile. Her heart ached with a renewed affection for this complex man who had walked through the fire of his own mistakes and come out the other side with a promise to right his wrongs.

As the applause and shared feelings of unity filled the theatre, Lottie brushed her fingers against Thatcher's for an instant, igniting a spark of connection that she could not deny. It was as if their hearts, once divided by secrets and misunderstandings, had found a way to beat in harmony, setting the stage for not only a magnificent play but also a new chapter in her own story. One she was very much ready for.

With the weight of secrets and deceptions finally lifted, Lottie found herself standing amidst a supportive and hopeful audience of her peers. Every single one of them knew of her writing skill. And they cheered her on.

Blast it all, but it felt amazing!

"Lottie, I want you to know that I'm not just apologizing for my actions, but for the way I allowed my own insecurities and pride to stand between us," Thatcher said.

"I'm not without fault either. I allowed my own fears to cloud my judgment. I should have trusted you more."

He reached out and took her hand in his, and she felt the warmth of his fingers against her skin. "Perhaps we were both too proud for our own good. But now, I want to make things right, and not just in our collaboration but in everything. I want to be honest with you, Lottie."

She squeezed his hand gently. "And I with you. Thatcher, there's something I haven't been entirely honest about."

He raised an eyebrow. "What is it?"

She took a deep breath before continuing, "I've harbored feelings for you, stronger than the collaboration we've been sharing. I've fallen for you. Completely and utterly."

A sweet smile tugged at the corners of his lips. "You've just described the very feelings that have been taking root in my heart as well. I love you."

The world around Lottie seemed to stand still, as if it were holding its breath in anticipation. Two stubborn souls who had weathered a tumultuous journey had finally reached a place of mutual understanding, honesty, and love.

In the theatre where they had once clashed, they now stood together as a united force, ready to embark on a new chapter, personally and professionally. Lottie just knew their love story was destined to be as dramatic and captivating as any play they could ever write.

As Lottie's lips met Thatcher's once more in a sweet, passionate kiss, their fellow actors and Rainville burst into cheers and applause. It was a moment of celebration and triumph, not just for Lottie, but for their entire theatrical family.

Lottie pulled away from their kiss, her smile as bright as the stage lights, and she knew that from this point onward, they would face the challenges and joys of life together. Her collaboration with Thatcher had led them to a love that transcended the boundaries of theatre.

"I love you, Thatcher Goodrich."

"I love you, Lottie Castlebury."

Time to script their own future, side by side.

EPILOGUE

L OTTIE STOOD IN the wings of Rhodes Theatre, her pulse racing with excitement and nervousness. It was the opening night of the play she and Thatcher had worked so tirelessly on, and the culmination of their transformation from reluctant collaborators to lovers. The theatre buzzed with anticipation as the audience settled into their seats, the murmurs and rustling of silk gowns filling the air. Lottie's gaze wandered to the elegant boxes where her family was seated, their proud smiles reassuring her. Her sister-in-law Sadie gave her an encouraging nod.

Thatcher stood beside her, his hand finding hers as they exchanged a glance filled with shared hopes and dreams. He wore a finely tailored suit, a far cry from the shabby attire of his struggling artist days, she knew, and his smoky eyes sparkled with warmth and adoration.

"It's going to be amazing," Lottie whispered to him, her voice filled with conviction.

Thatcher flashed her a grateful smile, tightening his fingers around hers. "Only with you by my side, my love."

As the theatre lights dimmed and the curtains began to rise, Lottie's heart raced. The play unfolded before them, brought to life by the talented cast who had poured their hearts into the production. Each line, each scene, exemplified the collaborative genius of Lottie and Thatcher. The story, a clash of beliefs and a struggle for personal freedom, resonated with the audience.

Laughter, gasps, and tears punctuated the performance, evidence of the emotional impact the play had on its viewers.

As the final act approached, Lottie watched from the wings, her hands tightly entwined with Thatcher's. They had been through so much together, from creative clashes to personal revelations, and now they were about to share the culmination of their efforts with a captivated audience. It was a dream come true. No, more than that. It was *everything*.

When the last line was delivered, and the actors took their final bow, the theatre erupted into thunderous applause. The curtain call seemed to stretch on forever, the audience showing their appreciation for the remarkable production.

Thatcher stepped onto the stage, his gaze meeting hers with a shared sense of accomplishment. Then, as if in a dream, King William IV himself rose from his seat, clapping slowly.

Thatcher, taking a deep breath, moved forward. He was greeted with more applause as he approached the King. When he reached the front of the stage, he turned to face the audience. "Ladies and gentlemen, Your Gracious Majesty," he began, "I am deeply honored by your presence here tonight. But I must take a moment to give credit where credit is due. This play tonight is the result of an artistic collaboration, and I would be remiss if I did not acknowledge the true genius behind it." He turned and extended a hand toward the wings, where Lottie had been waiting in the shadows. "Come on out and let them see you."

Lottie hesitated, then stepped into the spotlight, her heart pounding as she faced the audience from the stage.

Thatcher's voice held a tenderness that resonated through the theatre. "Allow me to introduce Lady Lottie, not only a brilliant creator but truly England's finest playwright. Her talents are unparalleled, and her contribution to this play is immeasurable."

For a moment, the theatre fell silent. Then, slowly, King William began clapping again, and the rest of the crowd joined in. The applause swelled, and the entire theatre seemed to vibrate with the force of their celebration.

Lottie stepped forward to stand beside Thatcher, her eyes shining with emotion. He took her hand in his and declared, "Together, we have achieved something extraordinary, and I am not only proud of our play but of the remarkable woman who co-created it with me. Lady Lottie, the love of my life."

The ovation continued, and Lottie tossed Thatcher a triumphant and affectionate gaze. The love that had grown between them during their collaboration was now on display for all to see, and it felt wonderful. They had not only created a successful play but had discovered love for each other, and to her, that was the greatest success of all.

As the applause continued, King William leaned forward. "Lady Lottie, please come forward."

With Thatcher's encouragement, she took hesitant steps upstage, feeling the warmth of the spotlight on her face and the gaze of hundreds fixed upon her.

King William cleared his throat. "Lady Lottie, you are a marvel, much like my beloved Dotti in her heyday. The creativity and genius you have shared with us tonight will be celebrated and remembered for generations to come. You have brought new life to the theatre, and I am deeply impressed."

The king's words filled her with a profound sense of accomplishment and honor. To be compared to his beloved Dotti, a celebrated actress and theatre star, was a compliment of the highest order. The theatre's cheers, coupled with the king's admiration, created a moment she would forever cherish.

As the standing ovation continued, Lottie glanced at Thatcher. The two of them had achieved something remarkable. Their future seemed brimming with endless possibilities.

Like the blank page of a new journal, just waiting to be filled. Only better.

⊰⟫⟫⟫⟨⟨⟨⊱

AFTER THE CURTAIN fell for the final time, Lottie and Thatcher made their way to the theatre's reception area, where their family and friends awaited. The air was filled with excitement and chatter as the cast and crew celebrated their success.

Lottie's brother, Crawford, and her sister-in-law, Sadie, approached with warm smiles. "That was extraordinary," Crawford said, his eyes filled with pride. "The king was thoroughly entertained."

As the royal party joined the reception, King William IV himself approached Lottie and Thatcher. His eyes twinkled with amusement as he said, "My dear Lady Lottie and Mr. Goodrich, your play was a true delight. I haven't been so thoroughly entertained in years."

Thatcher and Lottie exchanged a glance, their hearts pounding. "Your Majesty, we are truly honored by your kind words," Lottie replied.

"Well done, my dear." He beamed like a proud father. Then the king's eyes shifted to Thatcher. "And Mr. Goodrich, you have again proven yourself a remarkable playwright. I look forward to seeing more of your work in the future."

Thatcher bowed deeply. "Thank you, Your Majesty. I am humbled by your praise."

As the night wore on, and the revelry continued, Lottie stole a moment alone with Thatcher. They found a quiet corner of the theatre, away from the prying eyes of the guests.

"I can't believe we did it," Lottie whispered. "Our play is a success."

Thatcher brushed a strand of hair away from her face. "And it's only the beginning, my love. There are many more stories we will write together."

Lottie leaned in, her lips meeting his in a sweet, lingering kiss. Love and creativity had triumphed, and she was ready to face whatever the future held, hand in hand with Thatcher.

She smiled as their lips parted. "I couldn't have asked for a better partner, both on and off the stage."

Thatcher's eyes sparkled with affection. "Nor could I. You are my muse, my inspiration, and the love of my life."

"Write that down in case you ever forget."

"Oh, honey, this I'll never forget. I couldn't."

"Why is that?" Lottie asked, her breath hitching.

"Because your love is written on my soul."

Oh, that was good.

Very, very good.

The End

About the Author

Jennifer Seasons started her career writing contemporary romances for Avon and is the author of several popular contemporary and Regency historical romances. Born in California, Jennifer has lived all over the West and now resides in the mountains of Massachusetts with her husband and their children. A dog and several cats keep them company. A lover of autumn, cozy cardigans, and coffee, Jennifer can often be found writing her novels by hand in notebooks, bundled in said cardigan with a steaming mug of dark roast nearby. When she's not writing, Jennifer enjoys running, hiking with her family, gardening, and lounging in a comfy spot with a good book and a homemade chocolate chip cookie or two.

Amazon – https://www.amazon.com/stores/Jennifer-Seasons/author/B00D8GZ5EE
Twitter – https://twitter.com/JenniferSeasons

Milton Keynes UK
Ingram Content Group UK Ltd.
UKHW020727110724
445228UK00013B/491

9 781963 585780